ACTION
IN THE
NORTH ATLANTIC

by

Guy Gilpatric

ACTION

IN THE

NORTH ATLANTIC

by

Guy Gilpatric

FIRST EDITION

THE GLENCANNON PRESS

PALO ALTO

2000

The original text was published in 1943 by the William Byrd Press, Inc. of Richmond, Virginia for E.P. Dutton & Co. Inc. of New York.

Cover photo courtesy Imperial War Museum.

CIP Data is available from the publisher on request.

ISBN 1-889901-15-6

The Glencannon Press
P.O. Box 341
Palo Alto, CA 94302
Tel. 800-711-8985 Fax: 707-747-0311
www.glencannon.com

TO
LOUISE

PREFACE

There are books and there are movies. Normally, a book is written first and if it is popular, a movie is made from it. Occasionally, the process is reversed with the movie coming out and, if successful at the box office, a book is written based on the movie. With *Action in the North Atlantic* the book and the movie were released simultaneously in 1943, a year of dreadful loss on land and sea, but also in which the tide of war began turning in favor of the Allies.

But the movie, starring Humphrey Bogart, Raymond Massey, Alan Hale (father of Alan Hale, Jr. of Gilligan's Island fame) and Julie Bishop, and filled with patriotic images and an idealistic message, was an instant success. In fact, the book contained several photographs from the movie although the movie, in true Hollywood style, didn't follow the storyline of the book too faithfully. Of the innumerable war movies of the era, *Action in the North Atlantic* is one of the very few that focuses on the crucial role of the merchant marine and the supply ships that carried the goods without which the war could not have been won. Over half a century later, the movie is still popular and is carried in video catalogs. Many in the maritime industry consider *Action in the North Atlantic* the finest merchant marine recruiting film ever produced.

Guy Gilpatric, author of the popular Glencannon stories in the *Saturday Evening Post* wrote both the book and then the story upon which the screenplay was developed. In fact, he received an Academy Award nomination (Writing, Original Story) for *Action in the North*

Original poster for Action in the North Atlantic. *Warner Brothers.*

Atlantic in 1943 but lost out to William Saroyan's *The Human Comedy.*

That the story changed so much from book to film may be due to the involvement of so many people in the movie making process. Lloyd Bacon received directing credit, but Byron Haskin and Raoul Walsh each directed at some point without credit. In addition to Gilpatric, writing credits are given to A.I. Bezzerides, W.R. Burnett and John Howard Lawson. With so many fingers in the pie one can easily see how the ship changed from a C-2 to a Liberty and got a new name; a love interest in the form of Julie Bishop was added; and major elements of the book plot were deleted — Hollywood in action: take a good story and change it.

Ironically, this movie, so patriotic and inspiring to the country, was placed on the House Un-American Activities Committee (HUAC) blacklist in 1947. The reason was that when the convoy arrives at Murmansk, Soviet workers greet the ship with cries of "*Tovarish!*" — Russian for "comrade." Believe it or not, the HUAC considered this a subversive message planted in the script by communists!!!

Action in the North Atlantic has been long out of print and used copies are rarely found. We have reproduced it exactly as it was originally printed with two exceptions — the movie stills are not included and the type is larger to make it easy to read. See how many differences you can find between the book and the movie; you'll need more than one sheet of paper to list them all.

Good reading!

Walter W. Jaffee
Editor

1

IN the darkness of the wheelhouse, Captain Elder stirred in his deck chair and rose stiffly to his feet. Stretching, he stood for a moment behind the man at the wheel, glanced over the fellow's shoulder into the pale glow of the compass, and then stepped through the open door onto the bridge. Along the starboard horizon was a faint tinge of pink, as the first light of the sun seeped over the curve of the world. All else was night — the soft warm night of early summer. Out in the bridge wings, Elder could see the vague, motionless silhouettes of the lookouts, while the watch officer, pausing for a moment in his monotonous pacing to and fro, had rested his elbows on the dodger, cushioned his chin on his forearms, and stood peering into the gloom ahead. The only sounds were the swish of the wind through the stays, the seethe and slap of the water as the tanker plowed the gentle swell, and the ceaseless rumbling undertone of her engines, like an organ played softly in a great cathedral.

Captain Elder shoved his hands into his jacket pockets and set about walking the stiffness out of his legs. At the same time, instinctively and professionally, he fell to sizing up the possibilities of the coming day. The eastern sky, he saw, was rapidly growing brighter and, save for a few streaks of orange cloud, it was clear. What sort of weather lay to westward, it was still too dark to say. But presently he slowed his pace, tilted back his head and sniffed the air. He came to a halt at the watch officer's side. "Fog around," he grunted. "Fm-f-f! Get it, Mister?"

"Yes, sir. We've been running through patches of it for the past half-hour."

"Well, the main bank of it's somewhere off there to port. At this time of year, the . . ."

"Torpedo!" The hoarse scream came from the port bridge lookout. "Torpedo! On the port quarter! There! See it? There!"

With a bound Captain Elder was beside the man. He followed the direction of his tensely pointing finger. Perhaps a hundred yards away he saw the white streak. It was coming fast!

"Torpedo!" Simultaneously, the lookouts aloft, fore and aft spotted the streak and took up the cry. The shouted syllables overlapped one another, the combined effect sounding like the reverberation of echoes in a canyon.

"Full left rudder!" Elder bawled over his shoulder, his hands clenched upon the bridge rail. "— Hard down, Quartermaster! Jam 'er! Jam 'er, man! Oh, Christ! If we can only swing the stern around ..."

There was a blinding flash, a sickening shock, a clap of thunder. He heard shouts and the drumming of feet upon the decks. From somewhere deep within the vitals of the ship came an obscene gurgling, retching sound, as the thick oil gushed out and the water poured in. The sound was that of a sick giant vomiting ...

"God, hear that? They've blown the living guts out of her! Abandon ship!" Elder shouted. "Sound that whistle, Quartermaster! — All right, men, into the boats! Take it easy, everybody!"

But already the ship felt loggy. The way was off her and she was listing so rapidly that the two starboard lifeboats lay unlaunchable and useless upon the steepening slope of her side. The after port boat had been blown to matchwood; the remaining one was lowered and lay resting on the water. Seen in the half light, the rope falls which still connected her with the davits looked like clusters of grapes as men slid down them. Some dropped into the water.

"Unhook, Mr. Rossi! Get out from under, before the ship rolls over on you!" Elder shouted from the bridge.

"We're waiting for you, sir."

"Get to hell away, I tell you! I'm going around to see if everybody's off."

He clawed down the ladder, which lay at a crazy angle. Slipping, crawling along the slanting deck, he made his way aft toward the engine room. Before he had progressed halfway, he heard the deafening crunch and shriek of rending metal — felt an earthquake shock, then another and another. The bulkheads were going! Majestically, the ship reared up as does a horse trying to unseat its rider. Elder wrapped his arms and legs around a stanchion and hung on. Higher, higher rose the bow, until the great ship towered vertically, jutting from the sea like an accusing monument to man's inhumanity to man. Straight below him — far below him — was the water — a seething, oily cesspool which belched foul geysers as heavy gear and deck machinery tore loose and plunged down into it. Off to the right he could see the crowded lifeboat, the upturned, agonized faces. He saw Mr. Rossi waving to him. He disengaged one hand from the stanchion and returned the wave. Then he pulled the inflation ring on the front of his pneumatic life jacket and closed his eyes ....

She went down with a roar like the end of the world.

ACTION IN THE NORTH ATLANTIC

2

"**G**OD!" In the lifeboat, thirty-seven men spoke one word with one voice. Then, "Lay onto those oars!" shouted Mr. Rossi, the mate. "We've got to get him as soon as he comes up!"

"— If," muttered Larson, the carpenter, nevertheless pulling for all he was worth.

"Everybody not at the oars keep their eyes peeled!"

"Aye, aye, sir."

"There! Is that him?"

"Yes! — No! — It's only a can or something …"

Mr. Rossi stood up in the stern-sheets with the tiller between his legs.

"Any sign of him from there, sir?"

"Unh! There's so much junk floating around, it'll be hard to tell which is him. Just keep rowing ... Say, Carstairs! How's Klein doing?"

In the bow, the second mate looked up from the form which lay sprawled in the bottom of the boat. "He's bad," he reported. "I don't know what to do next. We've got a tourniquet around his leg, but it's still pouring out of him something terrible."

Fernando Ortega, the Puerto Rican fireman, bent over the dying boy, shook his head sadly and then peered over the gunwale into the oily water. "Well, the Captain ees down there waiting for him, anyway!" he sighed, consolingly. Feeling it proper to offer a prayer for the fleeting soul and for the one already sped, he crossed himself and fumbled for his rosary in the pocket of his shirt. For some reason, however, his fingers refused to close upon it. Puzzled, he withdrew his hand from the pocket and was annoyed, even angry, to discover that three of the fingers were missing. Hastily, he shoved the mangled member into his pants pocket and then glanced around him to see if any of the others had noticed it. — *Madre!* He'd hate like hell to have the boys see him wearing a funny-looking paw like that! Assured that none of them had, he fished out the rosary with his left hand, closed his eyes and proceeded to pray ...

"There! There's the Skipper! — He's just the other side of that grating!"

They saw a head so thickly coated with black, shiny oil that it appeared to be made of tar. It lolled back limply against the air-cushion collar of the life jacket.

"He's still breathing. Grab ahold of him, you guys! Whoa! Easy, easy! There, that does it!"

They stretched him out on the bottom boards and wiped his face. He coughed stranglingly, rolled over on his right side, gagged, coughed and gagged again. Abruptly, Mr. Rossi knelt astraddle of him, grasped him by the shoulders and turned him over on his stomach. "Come on, Captain!" he urged, gently. "Heave it up and you'll feel better!"

Captain Elder was violently sick.

"Fine!" nodded Mr. Rossi. "Hey, Carstairs, pass the whisky back here."

The bottle was passed from hand to hand, but by the time it reached the mate it was still dripping Cadet Klein's blood.

"Poor Bernie!" shuddered the mate, wiping it on his sweater and then uncorking it. "Captain! — Captain! Can you hear me?"

Captain Elder nodded weakly. "Everybody — here?"

"Yop, we all made it, sir!"

"Good!" He lay silent for a moment. "I ... was ... under ... water ... a pretty long ... time, w-wasn't I?"

"Yes, a long time, sir. Here, Smitty — help me hoist him up a bit. Come on now, Captain, take a snort of this."

The Captain drank, choked a little and blinked. Very slowly he raised his head and looked around him. "Hello, there, men!" he smiled. But gradually the smile gave way to a troubled look, the troubled look to a scowl; he struggled to get to his feet but was too weak to do so. His fists clenched and he commenced to tremble. "Where's the sub?" he demanded hoarsely. "Where is he? Hunh? Did the sneaking son of a pig show himself? Did he? Did he?"

"Haven't seen a sign of him, sir. He either stayed submerged or else he's over there in that fog ..."

"Christ, I wish we could stop this bleeding," Carstairs's worried voice came from the bow. "It's pretty near ankle deep up here, now. Parker's got his hand inside the wound but he can't seem to grab ahold of the artery."

"He's talking about Cadet Klein, Captain," Mr. Rossi explained. "When we fished him out of the water, he said he was all O.K. but when he tried to stand up, it was no soap. Then we found his right leg was pretty near blown off of him."

"No! Oh, hell," groaned Captain Elder. "Come, help me get for'ard to him, Rossi!"

"No, no, you stay quiet, sir. Carstairs and Cadet Parker are doing all they can."

"He's moving a little," Carstairs called back to them. "Sh-h-sh! Pipe down, everybody — he's trying to say something. — Yes, Klein! — What is it, Bernie? Go on, kid — we're listening."

Captain Elder struggled to his feet, stood dizzily on the thwart and with his elbows shoved aside the men who obstructed his view. For an instant, only an instant, he saw an ashen face with slowly moving lips. "No, Captain! Rossi restrained him gently. "Sit down and take it easy. There's nothing you can do."

"Warm! Warm!" a voice piped weakly from the bow. "It's so ... nice ... and ... warm!" There was a sound of soft splashing.

"He's — he's sort of paddling his hands in it! — In his blood" explained Cadet Parker, hoarsely.

"Warm! Nice and warm!" the voice was weaker, now. "Hey, Momma, this is really swell! Did the landlord raise the rent on us, or only hire a new janitor?"

"Jesus! — He thinks he's taking a bath!"

"Hey, Momma! — Momma! — Hang a fresh towel on the doorknob, will you? — Boy, am I having a swell soak! — Who says there's no hot water in the Bronx?" Cadet Klein laughed happily and, still laughing, died.

There was an interval of silence, broken only by coughing and clearing of throats. Then Carstairs sat erect. "Well, Parker," he said, in a matter-of-fact tone, "Now I s'pose we might as well get busy and bail some of this out."

Captain Elder gritted his teeth and fought back his tears. He felt that his strength had returned sufficiently to enable him to assume his professional responsibilities. He rose painfully and moved into the stern-sheets beside Mr. Rossi. For a moment he sat staring away at the great, slick patch of oil which blanketed the sea. "Five million gallons of it!" he muttered. "Five million gallons that could have helped win the war!" Then he shifted his gaze to the white, sunbathed wall of fog which lay a scant mile to leeward. "Oh, you Nazi stinkers!" he said, softly. "Oh, you filth! You — you ..." He spat into the water. "Well, Mister," he addressed Mr. Rossi, briskly, "We'll never get anywhere staying here! Nearest land is Montauk Point — should be about ninety miles, bearing about 297 degrees. If we miss it, we'll surely hit Connecticut. — That is, if somebody doesn't pick us up first."

"Right, sir! Let's get going! — Come on, you guys! — Ready? Give way! Stroke! — Stroke! — Hup! — Together! Come on, you shrinking pansies! — There's nothing so good for the liver as a brisk morning row!"

"— Liver, the mate says! Boy, what I couldn't do to a platterful right now!"

"Well, in just a minute, you can open your mouth and eat some of that nice, cold fog!"

"Lousy luck them krauts had to catch us out here in this clear patch, right against the sun. They simply couldn't miss us!"

"Yair — must have been as easy as smacking Goering across the rump with a bull fiddle."

"Goering? — Hunh! I guess you never seen my wife!"

"Well, I never seen her with you, Flynn!"

"Neither of you've seen her since she first seen my profile!" said Stanislawski, who stood six-feet-seven and looked like a lumpy mixture of Victor Mature and Frankenstein's monster. "Hey, lend me the loan of a comb, one of you lugs!"

"A comb, he says! Whatsa matter, Stanislawski — getting ready to run off a love scene with Hedy Lamarr?"

"Hell, I been ready for years!" smirked Stanislawski. No comb forthcoming, he smoothed back his hair with what would have been the lissom-wristed gesture of a gigolo, except that his wrist was approximately the thickness of a drayhorse's fetlock.

"Jeez! Handsome Stan! Look at him now, fellers! — Lights! Camera!"

"Aw, nuts to you guys!" said Stanislawski. "Just wait till I break into the pictures and ..."

"Captain! Look!"

They all looked. There, breaking the surface astern of them, almost at the spot where the ship had gone down, was the sub. She was heading in their direction.

"Maybe she hasn't seen us! Row!" barked the Captain. "Come on, men! — Hup! Hup! Let's try to duck into the fog!" But the submarine had spotted them. Soon they could distinguish upon her conning tower men who pointed and others who peered through binoculars; then more men appeared on the foredeck and stood grouped around the gun.

"He's going to shell us, Captain!"

"Then, by God, let's make ourselves hard to hit! Row! Hup! Hup!"

They saw one of the Germans in the conning tower wave the crew away from the gun. "What's the idea?" muttered Mr. Rossi.

"Do you s'pose he just wants to ask us some questions?"

"If he does, he'll get some answers he'll remember when he's frying in hell!"

"Say! " said Stanislawski, suddenly, "One of them guys in the conning tower's got a movie camera!"

"By gosh, so he has! You better get set, Stan — maybe he's a talent scout!"

"Turn your other profile, Stan! — Don't let him see that cauliflower ear!"

Leaving a faint trail of smoke behind her, the sub bore down upon them. Soon, they could hear the hiss of water parted by her bows, the pulse and throb of her Diesels. At least twenty men were visible upon her, all of them laughing, shouting, making obscene gestures ...

"Look out, Rossi! — He's — he's going to ram us!"

Desperately, Mr. Rossi shoved the tiller hard over. The lifeboat swung from its course. The submarine's nose veered with it. He dragged the tiller toward him until it crushed against his chest. Again, the sharp steel snout swung in a relentless, following arc, aiming for them square amidships ...

Captain Elder sprang to his feet. "Overboard, everybody'" he bawled. "Jump! Get clear of her diving vanes and propellers!"

The submarine struck with a splintering crash, cutting the lifeboat into two pieces which went bumping and rolling and tumbling along the sleek steel sides until they were smothered in the wake …

Kicking, thrashing, fighting beneath the turbulent water, Captain Elder's brain registered a single frantic thought — Get Clear! — Get clear of the vanes, lest they rip him in two! Get clear of the propellers, lest they chop him to mincemeat! Once, for a joyful instant, he thought he had made it; then he kicked against something hard and he knew it was the side of the submarine. He felt himself whirling dizzily; then he was swept outward like a straw in an eddy of a torrent and — blessed miracle — he was clear! Gulping the good air into his lungs, he saw that he was floating at the edge of a white highway which hissed and seethed like soda water. The highway was strewn with sickening debris, and even as he looked, red patches stained its whiteness.

A wisp of acrid oil smoke drifted down the wind. He turned his head. There, speeding straight on her course, was the submarine. Upon her after deck were men who laughed and howled and raved and danced with glee. The cameraman in the conning tower was calmly recording the gay scene for posterity ...

Automatically, beneath the water, Elder's hands clenched into trembling fists. — Sink his ship, ram his lifeboat, murder his men, make movies of the slaughter and ... *laugh*, would they? He raised his fists above his head and held them, tense and dripping, in the solemn, awful gesture of anathema.

But then, very slowly, they relaxed. And he waved at the little capering figures — waved cheerily, as though bidding them *bon voyage*. "Okay, boys! Dance! Dance! Jump up and down! Thumb your snotty noses! Enjoy yourselves! But ... don't forget, boys! One of these days, it'll be our turn!"

Mr. Rossi swam up to him, moving slowly, his face twitching with pain.

"What's the matter, Joe?"

"Nothing much, sir. — Guess I twisted my back a little. But some of the other fellers — oh God!"

"The ... propellers?"

"Yes."

"Well, let's raise a shout and try to get everybody together. If we start drifting apart, it'll be ..."

S-SHRO-0-0-F! Something rushed over their heads with the roar of an express train crossing a trestle. Instinctively, Captain Elder retracted his head between his shoulders. "Damn! They're shooting at us!" Warily, he craned his neck and peered after the submarine, expecting to see the muzzle flash of the next shot — or perhaps to be blasted out of the water. Instead, he saw a white geyser leap up beside her, poise there as though suspended, and then collapse upon itself in a smother of spray. And he saw that the little figures were no longer dancing on her decks but were scrambling for the hatches ...

He heard a muffled BOOM! from the direction of the fog-bank. Turning, he saw a destroyer come charging out of the depths of it, her forward guns blazing and white water curling out from her concave bows like fresh pine shavings from a chisel.

A cheer went up from the men in the water — weak, hoarse, piping, with here and there the sound of the death rattle in it.

WHOOF-F-F! SHRE-EE-SH! The shells were ripping the air over their heads, while all around the submarine, the sea leaped and boiled and steamed with the explosions.

"Come . . . on! . . . Come on! C'MON, you babies! — Sock 'er! Sock it to 'er!"

"Give 'em some more! Turn on the heat! Pour it on the bastards!"

"There! — *WHAM!* They got 'er! They got er!"

"Yes! Yes! N ... n ... No! NUTS!"

"It was too far to the left!"

"Look! She's diving! She's diving! Oh, Christ! Oh, holy Mary, Mother of God! Don't let 'er dive! Don't let 'er get away! No! No! No!"

As the destroyer approached them, no longer firing, she seemed to veer slightly in their direction. "Why, what the flaming hell's the matter with him?" barked Captain Elder. "Is he going to stop to pick us up? — No! Go on!" he roared, rearing up in his life jacket and waving his arms in frantic admonition. "Go on! Don't stop! *Don't stop!*" All around him were other waving arms and voices which shouted, "Don't stop!"

The destroyer didn't stop; she didn't even slow down. But just as she flashed past them she dropped two Carley rafts, and an electrically-amplified voice boomed, "WE'LL PICK YOU UP AS SOON AS POSSIBLE!"

"Atta-boy! Go get' em, sailor!"

"Don't mind us! Just do your stuff!"

"Say, ain't she a sight, though? And don't that old flag look good? — It's really somethin', ain't it, Mr. Parker?"

"Yes," said Cadet Parker. Very gently, he seized the body which floated upright beside him, placed his hand under the chin and lifted the head until the half-open, sightless eyes were turned toward the flag. "There, Bernie!" he said.

The destroyer kicked up a violent swell in which the floating men swooped up and down like corks. Each time he was at the top of a wave, Captain Elder could see the little ship circling, coursing, darting this way and that.

She was lobbing out depth bombs, now; they sailed up from her stem in slow curves, splashed into the water and, presently, exploded with muffled WHOOMS! which heaved up the water in columns like icebergs.

By the time the destroyer's swell had subsided, the vessel itself was several miles away and the intermittent booming of her depth charges came to them faintly on the wind. All who were able swam to the rafts; others, past help, were left in the water.

"We'd better hitch these doughnuts together," Captain Elder called. "Paddle a little closer and we'll throw you a line, Mr. Rossi. — Ready? — There, that's got it!"

The rafts were secured alongside each other. So crowded was his own that Elder had difficulty in finding a place to lie down. But he had to lie down. "Fifty-six years old and I got to go through . . . this! " he grumbled, wearily, closing his eyes against the blazing mid-morning sun. "By God, Carstairs — if I didn't know what a fine place the sea is in peace time, I'd call any man a fool who even went near it! Er — say," he lowered his voice, "— Can you figure just how many men we're missing?"

"I think we're shy eleven, sir. — That's not counting Klein."

"Klein is over here, sir!" Parker's voice came from the other raft.

"Eh? He's — he's . . . ? Oh! — You mean you brought it — you brought him aboard with you, Parker?"

"Yes, sir. I want to take him home to his mother."

Three Army bombers roared over them on their way to join the hunt and were greeted with a rousing cheer.

"Go on, you birds, git in there! — Drop some eggs on 'em!"

"Give 'em hell!"

"I bet they won't take no movies of you!"

For a while Elder watched them as they circled above the distant destroyer. Then, despite him, his eyes closed, his head sank down on his chest and he slept.

ACTION IN THE NORTH ATLANTIC

3

“**D**ESTROYER'S coming back to pick us up, sir!”

Captain Elder grunted and opened his eyes. Standing up, he scanned the approaching craft critically and — considering the circumstances — with a surprising lack of enthusiasm. Sailors were lowering ladders over her side; others were bringing blankets, stretchers and cans of coffee. It was all very precise, all very businesslike but, for some reason, Elder shrugged and sniffed.

“I'M GOING TO SWING AROUND AND COME ALONGSIDE YOU TO

WINDWARD!" the voice of the loud-speaker boomed across the narrowing space of water. "BE READY TO RECEIVE A LINE AND THEN TO GRAB THOSE LADDERS! ... DO YOU UNDERSTAND?"

Captain Elder stiffened. "Of course I understand!" he bellowed between his cupped hands. "What do you take me for — a dago?"

Mr. Rossi, on the other raft, shook his head and winked at Mr. Carstairs. "The Old Man's feeling his beans again!" he chuckled.

With perfect precision, the destroyer slid alongside them and came to a stop with her ladders dangling within easy reach. "All right, men — up you go!" Elder ordered.

"What about the sub? — Did you get her? — Did you get her?" they demanded eagerly of the sailors who helped them up the side.

"... Yes, what about it, Mister?" Captain Elder called up to an ensign whom he took to be officer of the deck. "Did you sink her, or didn't you?"

"We don't know, sir, but we're afraid not. There was so much oil that we couldn't tell whether any of it came out of her."

"Umph! " Elder grunted and spat into the water. From all around him came mutters of disappointment.

"Didn't get her? Aw, nuts! ..."

"Let 'er git away, hunh? Well, whaddya know! . . ."

"Say, what's the matter with you guys? ..."

"Er — Captain ..." The ensign leaned over the rail and lowered his voice, "That young fellow lying on the other raft. — The one the other boy's trying to pick up. Is he — alive?"

"No."

"Then ... I'm sorry, Sir, but we can't take him aboard."

"I see. — Well, you heard what he said, Parker?"

"Yes, Sir!"

"Sorry, Parker — mighty sorry!" the ensign addressed the lad. "Just you leave him there and come aboard. We'll — attend to everything."

"No," Cadet Parker shook his head. "No! If that's what's got to be done, I'd ... I'd rather do it myself!" He eased the body to the edge of the raft and let it slide into the water.

Captain Elder joined his men on deck. As he did so, he heard the voice of handsome Stan Stanislawski inquiring of the sailors if any of them could lend him a comb ...

"Now, then! "the ship's surgeon called out, "Is there anybody hurt? — Anybody needing medical attention?"

"Show him your hand, Ortega!"

The Puerto Rican withdrew it from his pocket and extended it, grinning sheepishly. "Aw, jeece!" he simpered.

"Wow!" said the doctor. "That's a bad one! You've had some pretty tough luck, feller!"

"Tough luck? — F-f-f-f! Ees notheeng! Here, look!" Ortega held out his other hand, on the middle finger of which was a ring consisting of two plump-bosomed mermaids who supported, between them, a phony 10-karat diamond. "Hah! Just looka how she sparkle! And just suppose am losing theece finger, 'instead! — What the hell the finance company say then?"

A sailor stepped up to Elder and saluted. "Captain Frazer's compliments, Sir, and he asks will you kindly see him in his cabin. — Just follow me, Sir!"

"Hunh? Well, my compliments to Captain Frazer, and you just keep your shirt on! — Mr. Rossi? Mr. Rossi? Ah, there you are! Mr. Rossi, I know I can depend on you to see that the men are well taken care of — that they get everything they need, everything they ask for. If you have any difficulty — well, just you send for me!" Then he turned, glowering, upon the sailor. "All right, you! What are we dillydallying around here for? Lead the way!"

Captain Frazer, who wore the two-and-a-half stripes of a Lieutenant-Commander, rose behind his desk and extended his hand. "Sit down, Captain, and help yourself to coffee and sandwiches," he invited, cordially. "I've got to ask you a few questions, so I can make my report, and then you can go in there and lie down. — Gee! I'll bet you're just about all in, Captain, er, Captain? ..."

"Elder's the name. David Elder." His tone was far from cordial.

"It's hard luck we weren't a bit nearer you this morning, Captain. We might have got him before he sunk your ship."

"It's too bad you didn't get him after he rammed my lifeboat."

"Well, we almost did! Some of those shells dropped mighty close!"

Captain Elder selected a sandwich, raised the upper slice and glared suspiciously at the contents. "It looked like damned poor shooting, to me," he declared, bluntly.

The naval officer stiffened and leaned forward in his chair; then the corners of his eyes wrinkled amusedly; he nodded and sat back. "You're quite right, Captain!" he smiled. "Any gunnery that doesn't hit the target is bad gunnery. Of course, we had the sun right smack in our eyes, and ..."

"— And if it had been raining you couldn't 've seen out from under your umbrellas. Yes, yes, I get it! F'mph! H'mph! But now, what I want to know is, when and where are you going to put us ashore?"

"Some time tomorrow. — Saturday. — In New York. Of course, meanwhile, they may send out a Coast Guard cutter to take you off. But the chances are that you'll have to put up with our poor hospitality until tomorrow."

"Good God!" groaned Captain Elder.

Frazer laid down the fountain pen with which he had been preparing to take notes of

Elder's statement and smiled a puzzled smile.
"See here, Captain," he said, "I don't know just
exactly why it is, but somehow, I seem to get the
impression that you don't, er, *care* for the United
States Navy ..."

"I don't, but why stop there?"

"Then let's not stop there! Come, come
— speak up, Captain! Get it off your chest!"

Elder shifted in his chair and gripped the
arms of it. "All right, Mister!" he said, tensely.
"All right — you've asked for it! I don't like the
Navy because I love the sea! I love the sea
because in normal times, it's the cleanest,
decentest, finest place in the world for a man to
work and live. — In *normal* times! — But
then," his right hand swept up in a dramatic
gesture, "But then, there's war, and out come
the navies! — War — and as soon as the navies
get to work, the sea becomes a filthy, oily,
bloody, hell! — Look out there!" he waved
toward the open port. "Look at that oil, that
muck, those chopped-up bodies! Do you
wonder why I hate navies? — This navy? —
That navy? *Any* navy?" he leaned forward,
glowering and with nostrils dilated ...

"Well, er ..." With difficulty Frazer concealed his amusement at this naive line of reasoning. "Well, I suppose there's a great deal of truth in what you say, Captain. But, granting that navies are an evil, aren't they a necessary evil? — And in any case, just what do you propose to do about them?"

"What do I propose to do about them? Why, I'll tell you exactly what I propose to do about them! I propose to get another ship, to go straight back to sea and help to win this war just as quickly as ever God will let us! The sooner we move the stuff over, the sooner we'll get the war over! And the sooner we get the war over, the sooner we'll get the Goddamned navies off the sea!"

Frazer was somewhat stunned by this tirade and at a loss for words. And so he only nodded, cleared his throat briskly and took up his fountain pen. "Well, Captain, let's get down to business!" he suggested.

Out on deck, the surviving members of the tanker's crew lay sprawled on blankets, eating, talking, or drowsing in the warm noonday sun.

"Hey, you swab-jockeys!" one of them addressed the sailors who were cleaning the breech mechanism of a gun, "If any more subs show up, you just call us!"

"Call you what? We been wondering just exactly what you was, all morning!"

"Oh, a wise guy, hunh?"

"Yair, they're all wise guys!" declared Stanislawski. "A little while ago, that doctor comes walking past, takes a look at me like I'm a freak or something and says, 'H'm! Remarkable gland case!' — Why, say — glands is the one thing I never had a case of in my life!"

Smitty, a meek-looking little middle-aged man who lay next to him, said nothing. He pulled up his sleeve, exposing on his forearm the tattooed likeness of a hula dancer. He flexed his muscles, causing the dancer to writhe and squirm amazingly. "Aw, gee!" he sighed, wistfully; then, smiling, he dropped off to sleep.

In the ward room Rossi, Carstairs and O'Brien, the tanker's third mate, were having lunch with Lieutenant Halliday, Captain Frazer's executive officer. Presently they were joined by Frazer himself. He wore the harassed look of one who has recently undergone an ordeal. When Halliday had introduced them, Mr. Rossi inquired, solicitously, "How's Captain Elder doing?"

"He's lying down in my room. Er, resting quietly. — I hope!"

"— You mean ... ?"

Frazer shrugged, chuckled and helped himself to cold cuts and salad. "Remarkable character, that skipper of yours! Whew!" He passed his handkerchief over his forehead. "Tell me, gentlemen — is he always so, er — so full of steam?"

The tanker officers glanced at one another. "Well," Mr. Rossi spoke for them, "Most of the time, Captain Elder's the kindest, most reasonable man in the world. But of course, like all of us, he's got certain ideas."

"Ha! Ideas like hating the navies of the world, for instance? — And how he's got to win the war to get them off the sea?"

"Well, yes, that's his main one. For awhile, I thought that all his talk about 'navies spoiling the sea' was only a sort of smoke screen he was using to cover up the real reason he hates them. But lately — I don't know — I guess it's kind of become an obsession with him!"

"But — what is the real reason?"

"His daughter," said Mr. Rossi, stirring his coffee. "Adelaide, her name is. She's the apple of the Old Man's eye! Why, he's simply nuts about her! — Always has her pictures all over his cabin, and always used to be bragging about what a fine voice she had. For years, he was allotting home a good slice of his pay every month so she could have the best singing teachers. — Yes, and I happen to know that lots of times he and Mrs. Elder went without things they wanted and even needed, just so's Adelaide could get the very finest training. 'But never mind, Rossi!,' he used to say to me, sometimes, when we were off at sea, or maybe sitting outside the Raffles at Singapore or the Café du Rhone on the Marseille Canebière, 'Never you mind, Rossi! One of these nights . . . one of these nights . . . we'll tune in the old short wave and the announcer'll say ... *And now, ladies and gentlemen, the next voice you will hear will be that of the lovely young, coloratura soprano who has flashed like a comet into the musical sky ... I know I need not say that I refer to Miss ... ADELAIDE ... ELDER star of the Metropolitan Opera Company, of New York City!'* ."

Mr. Rossi paused and refreshed himself with a sip of coffee. "And then," he continued reminiscently, "And then, poor Dave Elder would either invite me into his cabin for a snort, or else, if we were ashore, he'd snap his fingers and holler for the waiter, the barmaid, the *garçon*, the *muchacho*, the *kellner*, or whoever it was served the drinks in wherever we happened to be. Gosh!" he mused, half to himself, "Why, I bet I've drunk enough Scotch, Strega, Arack, Pernod, Vodka, Fundador and Raki to fill three tankers the size of the one they sank this morning! — And all to the glamorous career of Adelaide Elder!" He shook his head and sighed.

"But — what happened?"

"What happened? Why, *bang!* She got married! *Bang*, went the Old Man's dream! And — *bang* went his feelings toward the Navy! You see, she married a naval lieutenant — feller by the name of Howard Rockwell..."

"What? — Howard Rockwell? — Gee!" Frazer gasped in amazement. "Rocket Rockwell was just about the greatest halfback the Naval Academy ever produced!"

"I'll say he was!" agreed Lieutenant Halliday, reverently. "Why, if we'd so much as dreamed that that was Howie Rockwell's father-in-law, out there on that raft, we'd have given him a ten gun salute and piped him up the side! — Say, what do you know!" he addressed a brother lieutenant and two ensigns who had just entered the ward room. That old — er, that tanker captain we picked up this morning . . . he's Rocket Rockwell's pa-in-law!"

"Get out! No, is he?"

"Believe it or not!"

"Well, holy smoke!"

"Say, I certainly want to meet that old boy! ..."

Later that afternoon, Captain Elder was strolling the deck and inspecting the ship without enthusiasm, when he was waylaid by a young officer who grasped his hand and cried, "Sir, this is an honor! Howard Rockwell was a classmate of mine, and ..."

"Oh? Unh!" Captain Elder withdrew his hand and turned away abruptly. He had not progressed far, however, when another officer saluted and said, "I can't begin to tell you, sir, how proud we all are to have Howard Rockwell's father-in-law in our midst! If you'd only been there at Franklin Field, that day in

'38, and seen him make his historic seventy-five yard run in the last half minute of play, you'd ..."

"Umph! Well, my daughter saw him — worse luck!" Once more Captain Elder grunted and moved on. "Hell of a note!" he grumbled, joining Mr. Rossi in the lee of the deckhouse. "— In the Merchant Marine, you can sail seventy-five million miles and nobody's even heard of you. — In the Navy, you run seventy-five yards and you're famous!"

"What do you mean?" asked the mate. "I'm afraid I don't get it, Captain . . ."

Elder treated him to a look in which were mingled suspicion and sorrow, as one who believes himself betrayed by a friend. "All right, all right — so you don't get it!" he said, nodding knowingly. "But now, just you try to get this, Joe Rossi! — The next time I catch you letting any skeletons out of my family closet, I'll ... I'll knock your dam block Off!"

4

NEXT morning, awaiting them on the dock, were Red Cross station wagons loaded with clothing; representatives of the Seaman's Aid, of the National Maritime Union and of the U. S. Maritime Commission. Also, of course, there were pressmen and a newsreel crew ...

"Now, Captain (speak directly toward that microphone, please) now, Captain Elder, I wonder if you'll tell us, in your own words, about your harrowing experiences with the submarine?"

Elder cleared his throat. "It sank us," he said, and started away.

"Yes, yes — just a minute, please Captain! Won't you tell us exactly what happened then?"

"We got in the lifeboat."

"Oh, indeed! So you got in the lifeboat! Now, what did the submarine do when it saw you in the lifeboat, Captain?"

"It rammed us."

"Ah! So the submarine rammed your lifeboat! — I suppose it rammed you deliberately, didn't it?"

"Hell, no! It rammed us at full speed!"

"M'm, er, I see! Well, now Captain, what are your plans for the future? — Just what are you going to do now?"

"— Do?" Captain Elder frowned upon him perplexedly, as though the question did not make sense. "Do? — When there's a war on? I'm going to get another ship and go to sea again. — What did you expect I was going to do — take up ballet dancing?"

As one by one the tanker's survivors were interviewed, each said the same thing in the same matter-of-fact manner; "I'm going back to sea till we win the war." The only variation was supplied by Stanislawski, who added, "and after that, it'll be up to Hollywood!"

Rejoining his friend Smitty, "Well, kid!" he smiled, complacently. "How'd I do in front of the camera, hunh?

"You done fine, Stan! The only thing — what was you making all them faces for?"

Stanislawski nudged him slyly. "I was registering different emotions. — Gettin' a free screen test, see? ... Well, c'mon, now, Smitty — let's get one of these Red Cross dames to give us a lift to the N.M.U. Hiring Hall, over on Seventeenth Street ..."

In a little room off the office on the dock, Captain Elder and Mr. Rossi were changing into the clothes which had been furnished them.

"Where are you figuring to stop, Joe? — Just in case I want to get in touch with you over Sunday?"

"Parker and I are going to get a room at the Chelsea. We've got some suitcases checked there."

"Okay; if anything turns up, I'll phone you ... Well, now I'll just say so-long to the men, and then shove off."

"I bet Mrs. Elder'll be surprised to see you, Dave!"

"Yes, I guess she will. I only wish I could go home to her right now!"

"Hunh? Why — where are you going from here?"

"Over to the office, of course! I can't get a new ship in Flatbush, can I?"

After making his report to his owners, Captain Elder walked through streets swarming with the crowd of a New York Saturday noon. He glanced curiously at the faces, faces, faces all around him. Some looked thoughtful, a few appeared worried, but most were carefree and happy. "Funny!" he muttered, "They don't seem to realize that this corner's less than ten miles from the sea! — From the war! — From the front!"

Struggling through the mob that milled in the subway, he boarded a Coney Island train and wedged himself in an angle of the platform. As he did so, an express flashed past with a rush and a roar which caused him to flinch violently against his neighbor.

"S'matter, Bud?" inquired the passenger, scowling. "Dintcha ever have a train go by ya before?"

"Yes," said Captain Elder, meekly. "But did you ever have a shell go over your head?"

"— Hunh? Shell over my head — Ya mean I look like a toitle or an erster or sumpin? Well, say! If you wasn't such a helpless old punk, I'd knock yer ears down for ya! I'd ..." But suddenly the fellow saw kindling in Captain Elder's eye a glint which caused him to bite off his blustering in the middle. He paled. Precipitately, he shoved his way into the car, glancing over his shoulder as though pursued by wolves.

Emerging from the train, Captain Elder breathed deeply of God's good air and then headed up the tree-fringed street toward his home. The houses on both sides were small and unpretentious but uniformly neat and comfortable. — Uniformly so, that is, save for his own. His heart swelled with pride as he came within sight of it, for it looked just a little neater, just a little more comfortable, than any other house on the block.

"Oh, hello, there, Cap'n!" the postman greeted him. "— I thought you was off at sea somewheres!"

"No. I — er ... well, I'm taking this Saturday off."

"Gee! Pretty soft!" said the postman, enviously.

Elder halted midway up the path which crossed the little strip of lawn and considered the flower bed planted to one side of it. This was a special bed of his very own contriving; it was his pride, his joy and his chiefest horticultural jewel. To an eye less prejudiced, the arrangement of red, white, blue and yellow blossoms might have seemed without method, even slightly scrambled. But to him, its proud creator, it was exactly, unmistakably and beautifully what he had intended it to be — the shield-and-anchor insignia of the United States Merchant Marine. "Gosh!" he murmured, "When I planted 'em, I never dreamed they'd come up as lovely as this!" ... He stooped to pick a white flower to take in to his wife and when he arose, she was standing there beside him.

"David!" she said, "Oh, my darling!"

44

"Oh, my dearest, dearest sweet!"

She leaned back in his arms and looked up into his face. "David!" she whispered. "What happened?"

He shrugged. "Oh — why, they sank us. Then, they sort of — rammed the lifeboat."

She gave a little gasp and pressed herself closer to him.

"Was it — very bad, dear?"

"We lost twelve men."

"Twelve men?" He felt her stiffen in his arms. "Twelve — men? Oh, you've — we've got to stop it, David! We've got to! When are you going back to sea?"

"Soon as I can get another ship." He put his arm around her waist and, slowly, they entered the house.

Gratefully, he stretched out on the sofa. Mrs. Elder sat beside him and held his hand. "Do you want to tell me about it, David, or would you rather not?"

"Oh, what's the good? It was the same as any other sinking. Next week, or the week after, you'll be able to read all about it in the papers. Hunh! You can even see us in the newsreel, if you want to!"

She made a little gesture, as though dismissing such things as trivial. "No, I don't want to! All I want is to get this finished — over with — won! Nothing else matters. How could it?"

He patted her cheek. "My little sweet!" he said. "My own brave darling! Tell me, Mommy, how have you been?"

"Oh, busy! — Sewing for the Red Cross! Look!" She waved gaily toward a work basket which lay overturned on the floor, with spools, scissors and needle-cushions strewn around it. Then her face turned serious. "I was sewing, just now, when I saw — when I saw — *somebody* — coming across the lawn. I knew it couldn't be you and I thought — I thought it was a man from the office with ... Oh, David!" and suddenly she was sobbing, her face buried against him. "Oh, my Davey, my Davey boy! It's the suspense, the waiting — that's the dreadful part! At every footstep on the walk, every jingle of the phone, every newscast on the radio — my heart stops beating and just turns to ice! Wherever I am — whatever I'm doing — that cold, dark, terrible dread hangs between me and everything, else. It — it even gets between me and the sun."

"There, there — come, now, my precious!" he soothed her. "That — *thing* which you feel between you and the sun is exactly what we've got to wipe out! Life won't be worth a damn until we do wipe it out! Well ..." he grasped her hand and squeezed it, and smiled as he felt her firm answering grip "Well, let's hurry and do it, eh?"

"Of course!"

"At-a-girl!" He kissed her. "And now, what's the news? Seen Adelaide lately?"

"Not since last week. She and Howard are coming over for dinner tomorrow noon."

"Is she — are *they* all right?"

"Just fine! Howard thinks they're going to send his admiral on a mission to Europe, and of course he'll go along as aide."

"M'mph! That's good! They say travel improves the mind!" he said, grumpily.

"Now, don't start that, Old Jealous!"

"M'mph! Well, how about some lunch, then?"

"What would you like, Dave?"

"What have you got?"

"Whatever you feel like."

"I feel like whatever's the easiest to make."

"They're all easy to make."

"What is?"

"Well, let's see; there are some eggs and bacon; I can make a chicken salad; there are chops in the icebox, and some asparagus. What'll it be?"

"Anything you feel like eating."

"No, no! — It's up to you!"

"No, it's up to you."

"Davey! Decide!"

"Mommy! Make up your mind!"

"Oh! You're dreadful!"

"Oh! You're beautiful!"

"Well, come out in the kitchen, then, and watch me while I fix some bacon and eggs, some chicken salad, some chops and some asparagus."

"Okay," he said. "— But, mind you, I only want something light! ..."

They rose from the sofa, laughing, and walked arm in arm toward the kitchen. But halfway to the door he halted suddenly. "Look, Mommie," he said, "I think it might be a good idea to have Adelaide and Howie come over for supper tonight, instead of waiting till tomorrow ..."

"Oh!" she said, "Oh! So you think — you really think you may be called — very soon, David?"

He smiled at her. "Well, I just think it might be a good idea to have them come over tonight," he answered, pinching her cheek.

Action in the North Atlantic

5

T JEFFERSON CALDWELL, the negro pantryman, came out of the ◆ subway at 135th Street and stood for a moment blinking his eyes at the dazzling Lenox Avenue noon — dazzling, that is, in all save the tint of the local population. Heading north toward 138th Street, Jefferson looked down at his feet, which were encased in brand-new shoes. "Feet!" he addressed them, impressively, "Feet! Right now, you might have been struttin' the Golden Streets up yonder, instead o' this-hyar Harlem cee-ment!" He paused to consider his reflection in a shop window. He straightened his tie and smoothed his lapels. "Now, ain't that somethin'?" he chuckled, admiringly. "From now on, whenever

Ah needs a new suit, all Ah got to do is get mahself torpetered, and let them Red Cross ladies clothe me in the robes o'sweet charity!"

"Hi, B'rer Jeff'son!" a fellow church member greeted him. "Why ain't you-all out dere on de ocean in yo' steamboat, comin' to grips wif de forces of evil and helpin' us win de war?"

"Why ain't you?"

"Because Ah's doing mah duty right here on land! Ah's an Air Raid Warden, Ah is!"

"Sho', Deacon! — Ah reckon you mean you're the blackout!"

Turning into 138th Street, Jefferson looked up eagerly at one of the tenements. There, sure enough, draped from the fire escape outside a top floor window, was the American flag ...

"Home, sweet home!" he murmured, rolling his eyes in adoration. Then, bounding up the steps, "Ah jes' got time for a hug, a kiss and two po'k chops, and then Ah'll git back down to Seventeenth Street!"

6

HOLGER LARSON, the ship's carpenter, unlocked the door of his flat in Greenpoint, Brooklyn, and stepped into the dark little hallway. "Hey! Hedda!" he called. "You in, Hedda?"

His wife stuck her blonde head out of the kitchen. "Hello, Holger," she said. "Why are you here, Holger? Have you been getting sunk again, or somet'ing?"

"Yes."

"You speak like you are very sore about it, Holger!"

"I am very sore about it. To be sunk t'ree times is no yoke, Hedda!"

"Well, Holger, you know what to do about it!"

"You bat I know!"

She reached down for a bottle of *aqua vitæ* and poured him a little glass of it.

"Ah, poor fellow!" Impulsively she stooped and kissed his cheek.

He patted her on the back. "Have a drink yourself, my girl!"

Obediently, she filled another glass. He raised his own, clinked it against hers, and smiled at her through his scraggly, graying mustache. "May thine fair plue eyes see the last Gott-tam Yerman poil in his own yuices in hell!" he toasted. "*Skol!*"

"*Skol!*" she echoed. Again they clinked the little glasses and drank.

"Can I make you some lunch, Holger?"

"No. I brought a herring along with me. I got to eat kvick and get right back over to Seventeent' Street."

"To the hiring hall?

"Yes."

"Good! Sit down and unwrap your herring, Holger; I will bring you some *knäckebröd*. But ... why don't you take off your hat, Holger?" And she put her arms around him.

7

IN the smoke-filled hiring hall of the National Maritime Union, on Manhattan's Seventeenth Street, men were variously engaged in scanning the lists of jobs on the blackboard, standing in line at the window of the hiring cage, reading newspapers, or swapping news and gossip.

"Hey, d'ja read this notice here?" The speaker tapped his finger on a typewritten sheet thumbtacked to the bulletin board. "It says *'all seamen are insured for five thousand dollars, payable to their benefic ... er, beneficararies!'* — Yair, and it says if you git hurt and laid up, you draw down the dough yourself, two per cent a month."

"Well, whaddya know! I guess it takes a war to make 'em realize we're human beings."

On one of the benches, a man rattled his newspaper. Says here 'The Navy announces the sinking of a medium cargo vessel in the Caribbean. Three survivors have been landed at Port au Prince, Haiti' ..."

"Only three? Jeece! Them Germans sure leaned up hard against that one!"

"Well, there was only four of us picked up off the *Tallahassee.*"

"... And one o' them not worth counting!"

"Aw, pooh-pooh to you! Say — looka them guys just comin' in! — Ain't they some of the fellers that was on that tanker layin' alongside us at Corpus Christi?"

"Yair, sure! Hey, you fellers — we thought you was on your way to England!"

"We was, but we had a blowout!"

"— Sunk?"

"— And how! Then they rammed the lifeboat, the dirty stinkers! They ...."

"... Sixteen A.B.s! Twelve ordinaries!" sang out a voice from the hiring cage. "Two electricians! Seven firemen! Three oilers! ... Have your cards ready, please!"

Throughout the room there was a stir, a fumbling in pockets and the sound of shuffling feet as men took their places in the line. The dispatcher nodded at the applicant who stood before his window. "Electrician? Okay — let's see your card, please! Er ..." he frowned at it, "Er — just what is this name here, Buddy?"

"Sh - sch - schi - schick - SCHICKELGRUBER!" stuttered the applicant, a meek little man who wore spectacles, a moth-eaten mustache and a sprinkling of dandruff on his coat collar.

"Hunh? — Schickelgruber? *Schickelgruber?* Hell, feller! Why don't you change it?

"B-B-But ... I ... d-d-*did* ... ch-ch-ch-change it!"

"You did? — What was it before?"

"It was-H-H-Hi-Hit-*HITLER!*" said the little fellow, looking fierce. "--T-T-Tit ... f-for ... t-t-tat, you know!"

"H'm! Oh!" The dispatcher referred to his vacancy sheets and then wrote something on a slip of paper. "Okay, Bud — so you get the job!" he said, shoving the slip under the grating. "Be in the North River ferryhouse, Jersey side, at eight o'clock tomorrow morning. There'll be an NMU guy there to put you on the special bus. Next man! — What are you, Bud?"

"I'm an A.B.   Name's Mieczyslaw Stanislawski."

"— Hunh? Don't sneeze it — spell it!"

"M-i-e-c-z ...."

"Okay! Okay! I'll just write it M. Stanislawski. Boy, there's another name ought to be changed!"

"Well, I am gonna change it. — Yair; fer the screen! — Say, what would you think of Victor Voiture, hunh? — Or maybe Victor Mathieu? — Or ... or. . ."

"Never mind! Here's your slip! — North River Ferry, Jersey side, 8 A.M. tomorrow, Sunday. — Next guy!"

Stanislawski shoved the card and the slip into his pocket. "Okay, Smitty, you're next! Soon as you git through, let's ease up to Central Park and see what we can grab off, hunh?"

8

HANDSOME Stan Stanislawski and his little pal Smitty — the former garbed spectacularly and the latter in a dark suit, white tie and black hat (both outfits by courtesy of the American Red Cross) — were plying the waters of the Central Park lake in a hired rowboat. As is usual on bright summer Saturday afternoons, a considerable number of sailors of the United States Navy were doing likewise.

Stanislawski, at the oars, looked scornfully at the jaunty white caps in the boats all around them. "Jeece!" he said, shaking his head pityingly, "Wouldn'tcha think these dopes would stay ashore fer a few minutes, once they git the chance?"

"Yair!" nodded Smitty. "— Don'tcha remember, I said the very same thing in practically them very same woids when you and I was up here last time?"

"Yair! Er — er . . . Hey! Smitty! Quick! Git a load of them two dames over there in the next boat!"

"— Say! They're okay!"

"— Awright! Awright! Now, here's what we do! I'll row towards 'em, see, and we're pertending like you and I don't see 'em. Just before we crash into 'em, you yell '*Look, out, Victor!*' Then, after they stop squealing, you take off your hat and say, '*Sorry, ladies! I am afraid Mr. Victor Mature didn't look where he was going!*' — Just leave the rest to me!"

The collision was brought off successfully. Simultaneously, from the bottom of the other boat, there reared up a naval chief petty officer with the approximate physique and exact facial expression of Gargantua, the well-known gorilla. He snatched an oar from one of his damsels and made a mighty but futile swipe with it. "Scram, you lousy bums!" he roared.

When they had retreated a safe distance down the lake, "M'mf! Oh, well," Stanislawski produced a pocket comb, arranged his hair and then resumed the oars. "Welp, I s'pose we might as well go ashore and see if we can scare up something there."

"Yair, I guess we better," agreed Smitty. "You and I gotta find ourselves a little family life somewheres, between now and tomorrer morning! ..."

ACTION IN THE NORTH ATLANTIC

9

W ITH the chin of his bowed head resting on his chest and his hands clasped behind him, Mr. Rossi walked slowly through the misty, Neon-glowing night of West Twenty-third Street. His brow was clouded and his somewhat-saturnine face was deathly pale. From time to time his lips twitched and trembled, as though striving to express dark thoughts; then he would shake his head violently, as though bidding the thoughts begone, and freeze his lips into a thin, straight line. He looked neither to right nor left; he seemed oblivious of the city, of his fellow men and even of his own corporeal self. Here, you would have said, was a man who walked alone with some great sorrow, even as Dante walked the streets of Florence, mourning his dead Beatrice. As a matter of fact, however, Mr. Rossi was merely drunk ...

Now, Mr. Rossi did not drink often, but when he did drink, he *drank*. There was nothing gay or frolicsome about his jags; he did not laugh, sing, caper or stagger; indeed, the drunker he got, the sadder, quieter, colder and steadier he became. — Yes, and the deadlier! Thus, rapt in gloomy thought and heeding not the traffic lights, he stepped off the curb into Seventh Avenue. A taxi driver slammed on his brakes and came screeching to a stop, bare inches from him. "Wake up, louse!" he admonished.

— SWISH! Mr. Rossi's right fist whipped around from behind him like a cobra. — SOCK! . . . and the taxi driver went out cold. Without so much as a change of expression or a single backward glance, Mr. Rossi continued on his melancholy, somnambulistic way.

At Seventeenth Street, by a sort of reflex action, he turned into a saloon. Vaguely, he saw that the bar was crowded with men, but though two or three of them nodded respectfully, he seemed not to notice.

"Well, what'll it be, Mac?" the bartender inquired, wiping the mahogany with his towel.

"Six double whiskies and a triple one," said Mr. Rossi, sepulchrally.

"Hunh? Oh, quit yer kidding, Mac! C'mon, now, I'm busy! What'll . . ."

Very slowly, Mr. Rossi raised his head and looked the bartender straight in the eye. "*Six... double ... whiskies ... and ... a ... triple ... one!*" he repeated, but this time his voice was cold with menace.

"Okay! Okay!" said the bartender, hastily setting up the seven glasses and pouring them as ordered.

A hush fell upon the room. As though in a trance, Mr. Rossi took up a double whisky in each hand; then, left, right, GULP!, GULP! he emptied them in two swallows. Setting down the glasses, he snatched up the next pair and — GULP!, GULP! their contents vanished. — GULP!, GULP! came the twin sounds again and lo, six empty classes stood in a row on the bar before him. A gasp went up from the crowd. — The thing had been swift, mechanical, precise, like the working of a skillfully-handled machine gun! Now, they expected to see him cough, sputter, or perhaps go out like a light. Instead, they heard him murmur, dreamily, "Well, I guess I'll have a little drink!" and saw him sipping his triple whisky in the slow, conservative manner of one who restricts himself to a single snort per day and likes to make it last.

A wondering murmur went up, dominated by a note of admiration. "Jeece! D'ja see that?"

"Some boy!"

"Zowie! That's knocking 'em over!"

"Say, who is that guy? Know him, Stan?"

"Him? Sure!" said Stanislawski. "That's Rossi, the mate of the ship Smitty and I just got sunk on. He's quite a guy! Say, you haven't seen Smitty come in yet, have you?"

"Unh-unh!"

"Well, I wonder what's keepin' him? We — we kinder got separated, up in the Park. He was supposed to meet me here between ten and eleven." Stanislawski scowled up at the clock and then sipped his beer moodily, as though the day had brought its disappointments ...

Abruptly, Mr. Rossi set his empty glass upon the bar and fell to cursing softly. His voice was little louder than a whisper — sibilant, menacing, but as far as the present company was concerned, utterly impersonal. He seemed to be cursing someone far away, or someone in the dark, distant past. He cursed and cursed and cursed, blasphemies and obscenities hissing and tumbling from his pale lips like an icy mountain torrent from a precipice.

"Jeece, Stan — that guy's good!"

"— Joe Rossi? Sure he's good! Whad I tell ya? — I only wish I knew what's happened to little Sm ... Oh, there he is! Hey, Smitty! Here I am, Smitty! Say, you little jerk! — Where ya been?"

Smitty, whose face bore the imprints of well-rouged lips and who was carrying his collar and his necktie in his hand, rolled his eyes rapturously and took a long drag at Stanislawski's beer.

"Boy, did I need that!" he said, weakly but gratefully. "Quick — order one fer me, Stan — I gotta regain me strength!

"... Hunh? Why, say, you little disserpated runt, you! . . . What's happened to yer so-called strength, hunh? And what's happened to yer bankroll?"

By way of answer, Smitty closed his eyes, kissed his fingertips, then waved them airily toward the ceiling. "Gone!" he breathed. "All gone! Gone wit'd' wind! Ah, Veronica!" He hugged himself passionately and then helped himself to another swig of Stanislawski's beer.

"— Smith-h-h! S-S-Stanislawski!"

The voice was not loud, but instinctively, the pair stiffened and turned respectfully toward it.

Head down and hands clasped behind him, Mr. Rossi surveyed them darkly from under his half-closed eyelids, meanwhile swaying to-and-fro on his heels.

"Smith!" he said. "Stanislawski! — Stanislawski! — Smith! That sounds like four of you — but you aren't! No, no, no, don't get that idea! There are only two of you! There is only one of me, which is a damned sight too many!" He turned his cold, filmed eyes upon the bartender. "Well, rat! Didn't you understand my order? I said *SIX* ... *DOUBLE*

WHISKIES ... AND ... A ... TRIPLE ... ONE! ....
Come here, Stan! Come here, Smitty! You're
two damned good men, you are, and I'm proud
to have you watch me drink with me! Er, tell me
(GULP-GULP! GULP-GULP! GULP-
GULP!) . . . er, tell me, boys — have you found
another ship, yet?"

"Yes, sir!" said Stanislawski. "Me and
Smitty signed on pretty near as soon as we got
ashore. We gotta be at the Joisey side of the
North River Ferry at eight o'clock tomorrer
morning."

"Oh, yair?" A bystander put down his
glass and leered wisely upon them. "Well, I
guess you know where you're goin', don'tcha?
— Or don'tcha?"

"Sure, Bud!" said Stanislawski. "We're
going to Joisey City!"

"You're going to Russia!" said the
stranger, wagging his head knowingly. "You're
going to Murmansk! And how do I know? How
do I know? Ask me!"

"I ... ask ... you," said Mr. Rossi.

"You do? Okay — I'll tell you! If these
guys are crossing by North River Ferry, they're
going to Lemington. If they're going to

Lemington, they're going aboard one of them new C-2s. If they're going aboard one of them new C-2s, they're corning around to Hoboken to load some of them tanks and bombers and ..."

Mr. Rossi's ophidian eyelids flickered upwards for an instant. Within that instant, he caught sight of a sign behind the bar — a sign which read

A SLIP OF THE LIP
CAN SINK A SHIP!

"— Er, pardon me!" he interrupted, whisperingly, "Do ... you ... see ... that ... sign ... sir?

"That? Hunh! Sure! But . . ."

SOCK!

Mr. Rossi did not look down at the unconscious form; in fact, he did not seem to be looking in any direction at all. Even though he took up one of his seven whisky glasses and poured the few drops which remained in it on his bruised and bleeding knuckles, his eyes, like his mind, seemed occupied with dark, inner mysteries.

With the chin of his bowed head resting upon his chest and his hands clasped behind him, Mr. Rossi walked slowly out into the misty, Neon-glowing night of West Seventeenth Street. His brow was clouded and his face was deathly pale.

Captain Elder put on his spectacles, laid the case on the tablecloth beside him and proceeded to sharpen the carving knife.

"Well, well, well — and how's my little baby girl?" he beamed at his daughter, who was seated on his right.

"Oh, I'm fine, Daddy — perfectly fine! But how's my own darling Daddy?"

"— Yes, and how come you're ashore?" inquired Lieutenant Howard Rockwell. "Did they finally catch you tanked up on your tanker and fire you, Pop?"

Captain Elder glared at his son-in-law, around whose sprucely-uniformed shoulder dangled the gold cord and aiguilletes of an admiral's aide. "No, they didn't fire me!" he said. "— And don't call me Pop!"

"— But what are you doing ashore ... *sir?*"

"I'm carving a chicken! What do I look like I'm doing-milking a whale?"

"Now, now, David!" Mrs. Elder's pacifying voice came from the other end of the table. "— You know you really mustn't mind him, Howard. He's ... he had a little trouble at sea, that's all."

Lieutenant Rockwell studied his father-in-law's seamed and weather-beaten face and then nodded gravely. "Yes," he said, "I think I understand."

"Oh, Daddy dear! What happened? Please tell us!"

"M'mph! Oh, nothing much!" Elder removed his spectacles and polished them vigorously on his napkin. "Funny!" he grunted, "Can't see a damn thing through 'em!"

Suddenly, Adelaide reached over and felt the leather case. It was still damp.

"Oh!" she said, quietly. "They sank you, didn't they, father?"

"M'mph, well, yes — I s'pose they did!"

"— Oh, by George, sir! When did it happen?"

"— Ask Lieutenant Commander Frazer and some of your other — er, *fans!* — White meat or dark?"

Rockwell nodded understandingly. "You're right," he said. "Let's forget about it and keep this a family party! — Dark meat, please, Pop!"

"— DON'T CALL ME P ... ! Oh, all right, all right, Mommy! But I do wish you'd make him lay off that Pop stuff!"

As the meal drew to a close, Captain Elder leaned back and sighed contentedly. "Well," he said, "it's kind of nice to get home, once in a while! Let's go out to the parlor and sit around while Adelaide sings a few songs. — Gosh, baby — I'm really kind of — of hungry to hear you sing *Ben Bolt* again!"

Lieutenant Rockwell looked at his watch and then at his wife. "You tell him!" he said. "I don't dare!"

Adelaide Rockwell got up and placed her arms around her father's neck. "Oh, Daddy!" she said, "I'm so awfully, terribly, terrifically sorry, but I can't stay and sing for you! You see, Howard has arranged for me to sing at the Navy Relief Benefit tonight and ..."

"Navy Benefit? Oh, *Navy* Benefit, hunh? Well, it's too damn bad she can't sing for her Merchant Marine father's benefit, once in a while!"

10

W HEN the young couple had gone, Elder and his wife sat in their little living room, holding hands and listening to the phonograph. It was playing a vocal record of *Ben Bolt*, and though it was a pallid substitute for what he had hoped to hear, it was a perfect accompaniment to the peaceful, domestic and frankly sentimental scene.

As the last sweet note faded into the silence, Elder stirred. "If Adelaide would only ..."

"*Br-r-r-i-i-n-g-g-!*" the phone rang stridently. He took it up. His wife's hands clenched in her lap until the knuckles whitened.

"Captain Elder speaking! Oh, yes, good evening, sir! All? Yes? Yes? Well, say, that's fine! I'm — I'm really mighty grateful, sir! What's that? Oh, yes — taxi from North River Ferry! — Yes, yes, I know how to get there, sir! Okay — first thing in the morning. Right! Goodnight, sir!"

He turned and stood looking down at his wife. She stared at him with wide open eyes, her breast heaving gently. For a long moment they remained thus; then, very slowly, they smiled at each other. She rose and he took her in his arms. "Pack my bag, Mommy," he said, softly. "... My own sweet, pretty little Mommy!" He looked after her as she left the room; then he returned to the phone and dialed a number.

11

CADET JOHN PARKER sat at the writing table in a room in the Hotel Chelsea. The only light came from the little green-shaded lamp that stood upon the table, but it brought out in full the changing expressions on his mobile young face as he strove to set down on paper the thoughts which surged in his brain and the emotions which welled in his heart. He finished another page and read it, frowning. He crumpled it in his hand and cast it to the floor, where it lay among a dozen pages similarly discarded.

"*Br-r-i-i-n-n-g!*" He started violently at the sound and then picked up the phone. "Hello? No, Mr. Rossi's not here just now. Oh, good evening, Captain Elder — this is Parker speaking. — Yes, sir? Yes, sir? Oh, gee, that's great, sir! That's . . . *wonderful!* — At the North River Ferry? Okay, sir — we'll be there on the dot! You bet, sir! Goodnight, Captain!"

For a moment he stood smiling thoughtfully in the semi-darkness; then he lifted the receiver and said, "I want to put in a call to Glorietta, Kansas. The number is two-eight-seven and I wish to speak to Miss Mary Pollard. No, *two*-eight-seven ... Yes, that's right."

He moved to the window and, hands in pockets, stood looking out upon the city and the world ... But suddenly he stiffened and shook his head. "No!" he said, savagely, "No! I — I can't ask her, yet! — What the hell have I ever done? — What the hell do I amount to?"

He strode to the phone and snatched it up. "Cancel that Kansas call, will you? Yes — cancel it, please!" He moved slowly back to the

window and looked out again upon the city —
and the world.

"Got ... any ... iodine ... John?" Cadet
Parker wheeled. There in the doorway, swaying
slightly and scowling down at his skinned
knuckles, stood Mr. Rossi. "Who knows?"
murmured Rossi, as though thinking aloud,
"Who knows? The son of a gun may have been
poisonous!"

"Here — come over to the light and I'll
fix you up!" said Parker. "But, say, listen, Joe!
Get this! The skipper phoned a few minutes ago
and said he's got us a brand-new ship! We're to
meet him at North River Ferry at nine o clock
in the morning!"

"Good!" Mr. Rossi nodded solemnly. "It's
... damn ... near ... time ... we ... did ...
something ... about ... this ... war!"

"Her name is the *Merchant Mariner*,"
Captain Elder was saying, as their taxicab sped
along the highway which crosses the
Hackensack Meadows. "— She's a brand new
C-2 — one of those six-thousand horsepower
steam turbine jobs. — The Superintendent
swears she's a honey! She's passed all her trials

and had her shake-down run, and now they've got her back in the yards for a final check-up. — Well, I must say it'll be a pleasant change to have a new ship, after the — the ... Say, Joe Rossi! Wake up! Wake up! — And — and what've you been doing with those knuckles of yours, hey?"

Mr. Rossi, who had a hang-over, looked down at his lacerated hand, sighed, and closed his eyes again.

"Oh, now, Joe!" the Captain chided him, severely. "— Really, you know, you ought to be ashamed of yourself, always giving way to your nasty temper and going around socking people! — H'mff! F'ff ! — Fine way for a Merchant Marine officer to behave! — Fine example to set before serious young chaps like Johnny Parker, here!"

Mr. Rossi moved his tongue around in his mouth and grimaced. Obviously, he tasted unpleasant to himself. "— Christ, I've got a headache!" he croaked.

"M'mff! — Enjoy it, then!" said Captain Elder, relapsing huffily into his corner. But presently he saw on the border of the marshlands ahead of them a dark mass which loomed like a city. Over it hung a dense pall of smoke. Then the mass resolved itself into a forest of derricks and gantries; of rows of gaunt steel skeletons; of massive, plated hulls; of proud and mighty ships ...

"God!" said Elder, reverently. "Look at that! Look at it! Just — just *look* at it!"

Cadet Parker looked. His blue eyes opened wide and his jaw set. "It — it kind of makes you feel proud!" he said, quietly.

Mr. Rossi looked. His dark eyes narrowed and his skinned fist clenched. *"There's where we'll lick'em!"* he whispered, fiercely.

As they neared the yards, Captain Elder leaned forward and rapped on the window. "Stop at Gate Number Three," he ordered the driver. "— Pull up by the sentry while I show him our pass."

As they drove through the yards, they gazed in wonder at the row of great vessels which flanked their path, and at the swift, purposeful, grim and — yes, the *irresistible* activity in evidence on every hand. They saw steel beams and bundles of plates weighing untold tons travel smoothly past them on electric conveyors; — they watched torrents of sparks gush like comets' tails from the welders' torches; they felt the very earth wince and tremble as giant steam-hammers plunged down upon reluctantly-yielding metal. Perhaps never before in the history of the world had such vast resources in men, metal and money been concentrated upon the accomplishment of a single task. Compared to this, the building of the Pyramids was as a child building castles in the sand.

"Look up there!" Captain Elder pointed through the window at a flag-draped platform high on a scaffolding at the bow of a completed hull. "Look at that crowd, and the band and all — Say, we're just in time for a launching! Pull up, driver — we've got to get out and watch this!"

They moved under the forest-like scaffolding where, in the crisscross pattern of light and shadow, a gang of workers was impatiently awaiting the signal to send the ship sliding down the ways. From the platform above, the voice of an unseen orator came to them in a flood of eloquence — eloquence so distorted by a Corn Belt accent, an electric amplifier and the resounding acoustics of the hollow steel hull that only here and there could the words be distinguished.

"Bwah-bwah-bwuh-bwah-bwurp faw *Victawree!*" the voice harangued. "Buh zish to wahwah Axis domination? — Blup? Blurp? — Gaw-wah-wah? — No! No, I say to you! — A thousand times no! ..."

"Aw, nuts — don't bother!" one of the workers shouted upwards.

"Yair, button up, Senator!" urged another. "We gotta get the next ship started!"

"... Blupwah, buhwahwah the free-dum of the seas!" the voice continued, and from aloft there came a flutter of perfunctory applause.

The foreman of the gang looked at his watch. "Twelve seconds until ten o'clock," he announced, calmly. "Eleven seconds ... Ten seconds ... Nine seconds ... Eight seconds ..."

"Blah-wah, bublah blup Hitler? — No, nevvah! — Blup, on the other hand . . ."

"Ten o'clock!" cried the foreman. "— LET 'ER GO!" His arm swept upwards in a commanding gesture. There was an explosive thud, the resounding crash of falling struts and timbers . . . The ship trembled; then slowly, then faster, faster, she moved, she slid, she roared down the pathway toward her element, clouds of white smoke billowing from under her keel. She struck the water with a mighty splash, swam out upon it gracefully as a duck and then came to rest, swaying gently.

In the din of whistles, the blare of brass, and the cheering in which he took full part, Captain Elder saw the foreman stride to a blackboard at the top of which was painted a number; *Three Hundred Twenty-one*. Below the number, the board was ruled off in lines. In the lower line, after the words COMPLETED, TOTAL TIME, he chalked "*71 days, 4 hours, 31 minutes, 4 2/5 seconds.*" Then he unhooked the board and put up a new one headed: *Three Hundred Thirty-four*.

"All right, you lugs — hop to it" he bellowed to his gang. But already the men were swarming along the ways; already, the great cranes were swinging in the first elements of a new keel.

Deeply moved by the spectacle they had witnessed, Elder, Rossi and Parker walked in silence toward their taxi. But as they were about to get in, the Captain paused and viewed with admiration a ship which lay alongside the wharf beyond the road. — Sleek, new and four hundred-and-fifty feet long, she was; and though to a landsman's eye her squat funnel, jutting derricks and Samson posts might have made her seem ungainly, to Captain Elder she was a work of art, a thing of sheerest beauty. His sailor's heart glowed within him as he looked at her — then suddenly it swelled with pride and joy! For there upon her bow, he saw her name — *Merchant Mariner!*

"Gentlemen!" he cried, raising his arms towards her. "— Joe! — Johnny! — Boys! She's — she's OURS!"

Captain Elder led the way up the accommodation ladder with the bemused air of a bridegroom entering his chamber. "Gosh!" he was muttering, "Gosh!"

They were greeted on deck by a gentleman who introduced himself as Mr. Hannigan, the assistant yard superintendent. "Well, now, Captain," he suggested, "I suppose you'd like to have a look at your quarters and then take a turn through the ship?"

"My quarters? Never mind my quarters! Let's see the ship!"

And so David Elder inspected the *Merchant Mariner*, from forepeak to stern glands, from stokehold to crow's nest. Never, never had he seen a ship so staunch, so well-fitted, or in such absolute conformity with every one of his long-cherished ideas of what a ship — *his ship* — should be. As he passed through the crew's quarters and saw the comfortable staterooms with two berths, wash basins with hot and cold running water and mirrored medicine cabinets above them — as he looked into the club-like lounge room, with its massive reading table and deep, leather-upholstered chairs and settees.

"Welp!" he said, "It's hard for an old shellback like me to believe that all this is true! Twenty years ago we made our seamen live like pigs — in fact, their quarters were even worse than you can see on most foreign ships today. But this ..." he waved his hand in an all-inclusive gesture, "— This! — Well, I guess from now on, the world had better keep its eye on the American Merchant Marine!"

"Yair! And gee, Captain — just wait'll you see the terlets!"

"Oh! Why, hello there, Stanislawski! Glad to have you with me again! Any of the rest of the old crowd signed on?"

"Oh, yes, sir! There's little Smitty, and Jeff the pantryman, and Larson the carpenter and four or five more."

"Fine! A good ship deserves a good crew!" Captain Elder beamed.

The only time he appeared to be in the least troubled was when he spied the gun mounted on the poop. "Oh — a four incher, eh?" he said, lifting the canvas cover and examining the breech. "H'm! It's a late model — a new one on me!"

"Well, you won't have to worry about it, Captain!" Mr. Hannigan smiled. "This gun, and the .50 calibre anti-aircraft battery up there behind the bridge, will be in charge of a trained Navy gun crew."

"— Oh? — They will? Um!" Captain Elder nodded his head gloomily. "Um!" But then, suddenly, he stiffened and stood scowling fiercely. "All right!" he snorted, "All right! Navy or no Navy — the *Merchant Mariner's* a damned good ship anyway!"

ACTION IN THE NORTH ATLANTIC

12

TIED up to a dock in Hoboken, the S. S. *Merchant Mariner* lay loading cargo, and a formidable cargo it was. Captain Elder and Mr. Rossi stood on the lower bridge and watched the straining derricks as they hoisted up the various bulky implements of war, swung them inboard and then lowered them into the holds.

From time to time Mr. Rossi, who was supervising operations with a vigilant eye, found occasion to criticize, exhort or admonish the stevedores on the decks below. He did so with considerable fervor.

"Tsk, tsk! Mr. Rossi! Such language!" Captain Elder reproved him. "Now, let's see — where are you planning to load this other stuff?"

"Well, after we get the trucks aboard, I'm putting a couple more of the medium tanks in Number Two hold, sir," said the mate, consulting his cargo chart. "Those others, those big brutes, I'll distribute between Three and Four."

"Yes; we don't want to have her too stiff. And how about those crated fighter planes?"

"They'll go right here in Number Five," Mr. Rossi jabbed his finger at the chart. "They take up pretty near three thousand cubic feet apiece."

"And those big babies — those bombers — have you figured out how to make 'em fast on deck?"

"There are a couple of men from the Lockheed plant sent here specially to attend to it, sir."

"H'm!" Captain Elder nodded, musingly. "Those bombers ... they kind of make it look as though we were in for a pretty long trip, Mr.

Rossi! — If they were intended for England, or even for West Africa, they'd simply fly'em across. But ..."

"But — what's your guess, sir?"

"Russia!" said Captain Elder. "Murmansk!"

"Yes, it does look that way," agreed Mr. Rossi. "If we ..." Suddenly he broke off, clapped his whistle to his mouth and blew a series of shrill blasts. "YOU!" he bawled at the stevedore who was operating a winch at the hatch just below them, "Don't check 'er with a jerk like that! — What the hell are you trying to do, you ham-handed son of a ----- —? D'you want to strip the teeth clean off of her?"

Snorting fire and brimstone, he started for the ladder, but Captain Elder restrained him. "Oh, now, Joe — er, Mr. Rossi!" he chided, severely. "Oh, hey, now, see here, Mr. Rossi! — Really, you know, you ought to be ashamed of yourself, always giving way to your nasty temper! — That's no way for a Merchant Marine officer to behave! Why, I ..."

From the winch below came the crunch and snarl of stripping gearteeth. With a fearful oath, Captain Elder brushed Mr. Rossi aside. He leaped down the ladder, hurled himself upon the winchman and — SOCK!, he knocked the fellow cold.

"— I'll teach you to go busting up things on a brand-new ship of mine!" he addressed the prostrate form. "I'll … I'll …"

Snorting irately, he went up to his cabin. He was still dabbing iodine on his skinned knuckles, wincing somewhat and cursing to himself, when there was a knock at the door.

"*Come in!*"

The door opened and in stepped a husky naval officer wearing side arms and leggings. He came to attention and saluted. "Ensign O'Reilly, reporting with eight men and a truckload of ammunition, sir!"

"*M'm? Ouch!*" said Captain Elder, as the iodine bit into a fresh spot. He looked up sourly. "Well, sit down, sit down, Mr. — er, O'Reilly! — Don't stand there like a bloody Nazi storm trooper! I'll thank you to forget all that Annapolis nonsense, while you're aboard my ship!"

"Thank you, sir!" said the ensign, settling himself in a chair and watching the Captain complete his first aid measures with an understanding, even an expert, eye. "— Say!"

he grinned, "— From the look of your knuckles, sir, whoever it was you socked must have pretty sharp teeth!"

"Well, he's got fewer of 'em, now!" growled the Captain. "— But come! — What's all this about eight men? — And a truckload of ammunition, didn't you say?"

"Yes, sir. The men are the regular gun crew. The ammunition's for the guns. — Shells for the four-inch stem-chaser and loaded belts for the .50 calibers. You see, popguns like ..."

"— EH? — DON'T CALL ME P ... er, er, beg your pardon! Yes, yes, go on!"

"Er — well, I was about to say, popguns like those up there behind the bridge eat up thousands of rounds per minute. But if you'll let me have the keys to the magazine, sir, I'll have my men bring it all aboard and stow it."

"Yes, all right, but ... but just a minute!" Elder sat back and surveyed Ensign O'Reilly narrowly. He was, he saw, a good bit older than most ensigns he had met; also, he had about him the air of a man who has roughed it in tough places. Obviously, he was not one to stand for any chiding, riding or nonsense.

"Look, Mister!" he said, "As long as you and I have got to be together on board this ship, the sooner we understand each other, the better. Now, a minute ago you heard me mention Annapolis — mention it, may I remind you, in a sneering and derogatory manner. — I suppose you resent it. Well, if you do resent it, you can take your resentment and ... and stick it up your nostril!"

"Resent it?" Ensign O'Reilly threw back his head and laughed. "Why should I resent it? Maybe I don't share your opinion of Annapolis, but that's no reason I should get red-headed about it!"

"Oh!" Captain Elder's estimation of the young man fell. "— Oh, I see!" His lip curled slightly. "— So you'll let somebody sneer at your — *alma mater*, I believe you call it, and — and let him get away with it, eh?"

"*Alma mater* hell! The Naval Academy's not my *alma mater*! I went to Notre Dame! — I'm a Reserve officer!"

"Oh-h-h!" The disdain vanished from Elder's face and left it wreathed in smiles. "Oh! Well, now, that's different! You see, I happen to be acquainted with a Naval Academy graduate by the name of Howard Rockwell and . . ."

"*What?*" Ensign O'Reilly sprang to his feet as though stung. "— Howard Rockwell?" His slightly over-sized jaw protruded like the ram of an icebreaker. "— Why, just let me catch up with Howard Rockwell and I'll — I'll — I'll ..." Words failed him, but the two pile-driver blows which he delivered at the empty air were more eloquent than the entire contents of the dictionary.

Captain Elder stirred and raised his eyebrows questioningly.

"— Yes, Howard Rockwell!" the other continued, vibrantly. "— Romping Rocket Rockwell! Well, he sure went romping over me, when I tried to intercept that forward pass in the '37 game! He stove in four ribs and my collarbone and put me out for the season! Just let me catch up with ... with ... But, shucks!" Suddenly he tossed his head and laughed embarrassedly, "I hope you'll excuse me for busting out this way, sir!"

"Mmph? Well, all right, Mr. O'Reilly — I'm not interested in your personal feuds! —

Just get that ammunition stowed and I'll see that your quarters are ready for you."

When the ensign had gone, Captain Elder leaned back in his chair and scowled up at the deckhead. Evidently, he was the prey of conflicting emotions.

"Lick Howard Rockwell? — Him? Hunh — I'd like to see him try it! Still, maybe he could! — Boy, it would make a pretty good scrap, all right! And after all, what would I care who won? It'd be Navy *versus* Navy, and if they knocked each other's blocks off, so much the merrier! — But no! Howard's Adelaide's husband! — Howard's my son-in-law! Why, this fellow couldn't possibly lick him! But still ... but still ..."

Muttering to himself and shaking his head, Captain Elder plastered a strip of gauze on his knuckles and rejoined Mr. Rossi on the bridge.

13

NEW YORK became a smoke smudge, Long Island a low gray cloud; then they vanished below the horizon, and the S.S. *Merchant Mariner* was alone in her element.

"What's she doing?"

"Fourteen knots, sir!"

Captain Elder strolled to the chart room and joined Mr. Rossi and Mr. Blair, the second mate, beside the table. The latter was busy with dividers and parallel rules.

"M'mph! Halifax!" Elder grunted. "Why in hell are they sending us to Halifax?" The question was purely rhetorical; he knew the answer only too well. But Mr. Blair, who was an earnest young man, felt himself called upon to answer.

"Why, I s'pose we're going to Halifax to join a convoy, sir! They always ..."

"Well, don't you think I know it? But what've we got to join a convoy for, hunh? Haven't we got all these guns and Navy nuisances aboard so's we can defend ourselves? — If we can defend ourselves, what's the sense of joining a convoy? — And if we can't, what's the sense of the guns?"

He walked out into the wing of the bridge and scowled aft. He saw two bluejackets standing watch by the anti-aircraft guns while others, similarly alert, were at their stations around the stern-chaser. Ensign O'Reilly, on the gun platform, appeared to be giving instructions to a group of the vessel's civilian crew who were standing below.

"He asked me for seven men to handle ammunition up from the magazine," Mr. Rossi explained, joining Elder. "— Looks like he's going to put 'em through a practice drill or something."

As they watched, O'Reilly posted several of the men at intervals along the deck and dispatched the others below. Then he consulted his wristwatch and barked an order into the telephone. In an unbelievably short space of time, a man dashed out of the tween-decks with a long, slim brass-and-steel cartridge in his arms. He ran aft with it to the next man (it was Stanislawski) who snatched it from him as though it were the baton in a relay race. "Rush order for a gennelman in a hurry!" he shouted. "Make it snappy!" With a mighty heave, he tossed the shell through the air to the last man in the line. The weight of the missile brought the fellow to his knees but somehow he prevented it from striking the deck. "Okay! One rush order coming up" he called, passing the shell to the platform.

Elder saw Ensign O'Reilly mop the sweat from his brow — saw him summon Stanislawski to the platform and unburden his soul on the subject of playing pitch-and-toss with high-explosive ammunition.

"Hunh-hunh!" chuckled the Skipper, delightedly. "— Looks like our Merchant Marine lads are a bit too fast for the Navy, Mr. Rossi. Well, now, let's just have a little private drill of our own!" He entered the wheelhouse and spoke into the engine room telephone. "Give her all she's got, Mr. Clark!" he ordered. "Crowd it to 'er!"

He felt the pulse-beat of the engines quicken beneath his feet — felt the vessel's hull tremble as she accelerated her pace through the water. Heavily loaded as she was, her bow lifted but slightly as it met the easy surge; rather, she plowed straight through, buffeting out the spray in white sheets which glowed in the sunshine with all the colors of the rainbow. Glancing over the side and apparently satisfied that the ship was doing her maximum, Elder turned to the helmsman. "All right — let me take her for a minute!" he said, grasping the wheel. Abruptly, almost brutally, he gave her full right rudder. The steering-engine chattered and her stem slewed sideways, piling up the water against her port quarter. She heeled over and went into the turn. He crowded her around the full three hundred and sixty degrees, her churned-up wake leaving a milky circle behind her. Just as her bow plunged through it at the joining, Elder spun the wheel in the opposite direction and around she went to the left. He held her in the circle until the wake again crossed itself, leaving a great white figure eight inscribed upon the surface of the sea. Nodding in satisfaction, he put the ship back on the course and relinquished the wheel to the helmsman. "She handles as sweet as a dinghy!" he announced, proudly.

Aft on the gun platform, Gunner's Mate 2nd Class Hyman Goldberg looked back at the wake and then turned to Seaman 1st Class Alonzo Fitch. "What the hell's he trying to do?" he demanded. "— Invent a new design for a pretzel or somethin'?"

"Reckon he thinks he's ridin' in a rodeo," opined Fitch, who hailed from the Panhandle of Texas.

Just then, Captain Elder grasped the handle of the engine room telegraph and jammed it from FULL AHEAD to FULL ASTERN. Before the bell had ceased clanging below, the *Merchant Mariner* was trembling like a leaf as her full six thousand horsepower battled against her terrific forward momentum. Her lashing propeller blades heaved up torrents of suds; she creaked and groaned and rattled under the strain. Then the great blades bit into solid water and lo, she was moving backwards!

"Fine! Fine!" beamed Captain Elder, shoving the telegraph to STOP, then to SLOW AHEAD and finally to FULL AHEAD. "Now, I'll just try her on some zigzags!"

At supper that evening, after the *Merchant Mariner's* manoueverability had been admiringly discussed by those of her officers who were present, Ensign O'Reilly cleared his throat.

"Yes, she seems to have what it takes, all right!" he conceded, hesitantly. "The only thing is, er ... Well, frankly, Captain, that first sudden change in course gave us quite a start! For a minute, we didn't know whether you were dodging a submarine, or what! I wonder if in future you'd mind just phoning back to warn us?"

Captain Elder gave him a withering look. "Next time or any time I jam this ship off its course, it won't be to *dodge* a submarine — get that, Mister? And as for me phoning you ... well, I don't even know your number, dearie!"

From behind the Captain's shoulder, Mr. Rossi winked at Ensign O'Reilly. Ensign O'Reilly grinned and returned the wink.

But next day at noon, as the Skipper, Mr. Blair and Cadet Parker were shooting the sun, there came a shattering explosion which shook the ship and nearly caused Elder to drop his sextant. He dashed into the wing of the bridge just as the gun cut loose a second WHAM! Half a mile astern he saw a dark floating object; suddenly it soared into the air at the top of a spouting white column of water, for all the world like one of the little silver balls in a Coney Island shooting gallery. In the instant it hung there, he recognized it as an empty oil drum; then it fell, and almost as it splashed the surface, a third shell struck it direct and blew it to smithereens.

"Gosh! Some shooting!" cried Mr. Blair.

"— I'll say!" agreed John Parker. "Those boys are *good!*"

"M'mph!" grunted Captain Elder, his brow beetling and his neck flushed a deep red. He strode to the phone and flipped the dial to the gun-platform number. "Hey, O'Reilly!" he roared into the transmitter, "Next time you go

monkeying with that gun, notify me in advance!
— Understand?"

"You've got the wrong number, dearie!
— Excuse it, puh-lease!" a honeyed voice came
back to him.

14

FIRST, a big, long-range Canadian flying boat came lumbering out of the haze, circled the *Merchant Mariner* twice and then, apparently satisfied, droned off about its business. It was followed at intervals by smaller seaplanes and land-based aircraft. An ancient ex-American destroyer and a corvette appeared for a closer inspection. Finally, with the gray-green coastline showing above the horizon, the pilot came aboard to take her in through the mine-fields.

The vessel waited for the submarine guard-net to open and then steamed slowly into the entrance of that great marine amphitheatre which is Halifax harbor. Off to the left, dominated by the old stone Citadel, was the thriving, teeming town, its wharves piled high with munitions and the railway sidings behind them crowded with puffing, rumbling freight trains. But it was not the town which compelled attention, it was the harbor — the harbor, with its scores of ships, its endless rows of ships — its vast gray armada of tankers, freighters, transports; of war craft of every type from humble minesweeper to mighty battlewagon, brave with the flags of all the United Nations. Beholding them, one felt that Victory itself lay waiting here on the deep, placid waters of this drowned valley between the Nova Scotian hills. — Waiting, yes, but straining at its anchor ...

Mr. Rossi, at his station on the fo'c'sle head, viewed the spectacle through narrowed eyes. "Ships!" he muttered, his thin lips drawn back from his teeth. "Ships!" He pounded his fist upon the windlass. "— Ships! — *Ships!* SHIPS! ... Well, by God, it's by ships that we'll lick 'em! Yes — By God, by men and by ships! — That's how we'll win the war!"

A speedboat put off from shore, came squattering between the rows of ships like a taxicab passing through city streets, and brought up at the *Merchant Mariner's* ladder. An American Naval Lieutenant came up the side and was ushered to Captain Elder on the bridge.

"Sir," he said, "The Convoy Commander presents his compliments and requests that you accompany me ashore."

"Ashore? Why, shucks — I've been all over Halifax a hundred times!"

"No doubt, sir! But you're the last ship in, and the conference is scheduled in half an hour."

"Oh, a chinfest, eh? Well, all right, Mister. — Lead the way!"

Arrived on shore, the Lieutenant escorted Elder up a side street to what appeared once to have been a schoolhouse; now, however, the Stars and Stripes hung above its doorway and the sidewalk before it was patrolled by steel-helmeted United States Marines. Within the lobby was a table behind which sat several officers and yeomen; Elder was asked to identify himself and his ship and then was handed a slip on which was the number: Fifty-eight.

"This way, sir!"

He found himself in a crowded classroom the walls of which were panelled with blackboards. Seated at the rows of little desks were not bright-eyed Canadian school children, but elderly, florid and portly sea captains of a dozen nationalities. They bulged over the edges of their benches, they fumbled with thick, unaccustomed fingers among their pencils and notebooks, and stuffed their dead cigar butts into the dried-up inkwells before them. Several, apparently succumbing to the nostalgia for boyhood engendered by their surroundings, were passing the time by throwing spit-balls ...

"*Tiens, Capitaine Elder! Alors, comment ça va mon vieux?* Okay?"

"Fine! Fine! How are you, Captain Le Prieur? Oh, and there's Captain Vanderhoven! — Well, well, well! — How goes it, Van?"

"Ach, well enough! Glad to haff you with us, Elder! — Say, did you see old Captain Papadoulos sitting over there in the second row?"

"— Nick Papadoulos? — Where? — Oh, sure! — Hello, there, Nick! — How's Cornelia? How's little Miltiades? — Say, after we get through here, let's all get to — ..."

"Gentlemen! Good afternoon!" A Navy captain tapped his pencil on the rostrum and then paused for silence. "Gentlemen! I have the distinguished honor of presenting Rear Admiral Thomas Hartridge, United States Navy, your Convoy Commander. Admiral Hartridge!" He stepped aside and bowed to a pink-faced, blue-eyed old gentleman who wore the broad gold stripes of his rank and three rows of decorations, including the azure white-starred ribbon of the Congressional Medal of Honor. There was a shuffling sound as seventy-three sturdy merchant captains rose respectfully, if ponderously, to their feet.

"Thank you, gentlemen! Please be seated! Kerhumpf! Ker-hem! Well, gentlemen, the ships of this convoy designated as Convoy Two-Eleven, will put to sea tomorrow at the respective times which will be given you individually in sealed orders at the close of this meeting. Immediately upon weighing anchor, each ship will display its number, as shown on the slips now in your possession, by means of a hoist of flags of the International Signal Code. You will proceed directly to the point of rendezvous, the coordinates of which will also be designated in your sealed orders. There you will assume your convoy positions according to your numbers, as shown on this diagram. — Kerhuff!"

He took up a pointer and turned to the blackboard, on which was chalked

BASIC FORMATION
CONVOY No. 211

1	2	3	4	5	6	7	8	9	10
11	12	13	14	15	16	17	18	19	20
21	22	23	24	25	26	27	28	29	30
31	32	33	34	35	36	37	38	39	40
41	42	43	44	45	46	47	48	49	50
51	52	53	54	55	56	57	58	59	60
61	62	63	64	65	66	67	68	69	70
71	72	73							

"Now, you will please observe, gentlemen, that our convoy consists of seventy-three vessels, not including the naval escort. Normally, we will proceed in the formation shown here, spaced as closely as visibility and general conditions permit. In order to take your position, or to recognize and regain it if you lose it, you have only to match your own number with those of the ships around you. Thus, if your number is 36, the first numbers of the two ships abeam of you must be 3 and the first numbers of the ships fore and aft of you must be 2 and 4. respectively. Is that clear?"

There was a pause, then an assenting rumble of voices arose from the merchant skippers.

"Good! — But now let us suppose that, due to enemy attack or other causes, we are suddenly forced to alter our course Ninety degrees to port. — What then? Why, then, Ship Number 36 will have 6's abeam of him and 5 and 7 fore and aft. It follows, naturally, that if the change of course is Ninety degrees starboard, he'll have 7 ahead and 5 astern."

"— *Jesu Cristo!*" came a plaintive voice from the back row. "Ees complicate!"

Admiral Hartridge smiled benignly in its direction. "Ah, yes, ker-hem! I realize that all this may sound a trifle involved to some of our, er, gallant allies, ker-haff, but we have arranged to have it explained to them by interpreters, directly after the meeting. — Er, ker-hem!" he referred to his notes. "Er, naturally, the strictest radio silence must be maintained, although your receivers should be in operation and manned at all times. Inter-convoy communication will be maintained by four means, to wit: blinker lamp, whistle, flag and, when practicable, loud speaker."

The Admiral took a drink of water.

"A-hapf! And now, gentlemen, we come to the matter of enemy attack. Although most of you are armed, it is not always possible, in a closely-spaced convoy, to bring your guns to bear without danger of hitting a neighboring ship; therefore, the main responsibility for our defense will always rest with our naval escort. Your chief concern must always be to hold your proper position — to keep the convoy intact. However ..." he pursed his lips and spread his hands, "However, I know it is unnecessary to remind you that through engine failure, weather conditions, enemy action or what-not, you may become separated from the convoy. — The entire convoy may be scattered, even! Well," he shrugged, "In that case, it's every man for himself — or rather I should say, it's every ship for Murmansk! Yes, gentlemen!" he banged the rostrum with his fist, "— *Head for Murmansk! Your cargoes must get through!*" He stood for a moment looking down at them, to make certain that the gravity of his words was fully realized.

"And now," he resumed, "I shall touch briefly upon my own functions as Convoy Commander. My command ship, the S.S. *Cortez,* 22,000 tons, formerly of the Antilles-Caribbean Line, can readily be identified by its size. It will carry the signal Number 00 — double zero. Its normal position in the convoy will be slightly ahead of ship No. 5, and it should be watched for signals at all times. In the event of the convoy changing course, as described to you a few moments ago, I shall take up position ahead of Ship No. 51, if the change is to port, or ahead of No. 50, if the change is to starboard. Note that I will always be ahead of a *Five.* — Er — just let me make that clear ..." He took up a piece of chalk and drew curving arrows around the diagram to indicate the shifts in position.

"Ker-hem!" he smiled, a faraway look in his eyes, "— Looks rather like a diagram of a football play, doesn't it, gentlemen? — A run around right end! — Yes, it might actually be a diagram of Rocket Rockwell's famous run in the Army-Navy game in '39, when he ... Eh? — What's that? What did you say, Captain?"

"Nothing, sir!" said Elder, reddening.

"Oh, come, Captain! Yes, you did!" Admiral Hartridge beamed down upon him with the cordial *bonhomie* of one football fan for another. "Please speak up! What was it you said, er, Captain, er Captain Number Fifty-eight?"

Elder felt that all eyes in the room were turned upon him. "I said *damn!*" he confessed, challengingly.

"Ah?" The Admiral raised his eyebrows. "And why did you say damn, Captain?"

"Rocket Rockwell is my son-in-law!"

"— Indeed? — Indeed? Well, Captain," Admiral Hartridge was no longer beaming and his tone was cold and severe, "I don't know whether you're trying to belittle a great football hero or to capitalize on your family relationship with him. Whatever the case, I feel that your bringing up the subject at this time is in distinctly, er, questionable taste! Ker-huff! Ker-hem!"

"— Futboll? — Family?" came the plaintive voice from the back bench. *"Jesu Cristo!* — Ees eet of convoy he ees spikking, or yes, no? What ees now all theece futbolls and families, hey?"

As the Convoy Conference adjourned, Halifax, that incongruous combination of dingy red brick English village and concrete New World boom town, was limbering up for the evening. The streets were crowded. As Elder and his friends left the schoolhouse and headed for the Queen's Hotel, they saw the uniforms of the United States, Britain, Free France, Norway and Poland. They saw white men, red men, black men; men in kilts and men in fezzes; Chinese, Malays, lascars; Sikhs who wore green turbans and black spade beards, whose eyes were like smouldering coals and whose noses were hooked like the fierce beaks of hawks. The polyglot sound was like that at the building of Babel.

"Vous avez été blessé, alors?"

"Et comment! Deux fois, au ventre et au bras! Et dans le ventre, il y a encore deux morceaux d'obus ..."

115

"... And so I says to 'im, I says, 'Now look 'ere, yer bleddy tout, ye're talking to a gempman!' And with that I grabs 'im by the throat, I does, and I bumps 'is narsty 'ead on the sidewalk ..."

The dining-room of the Queens was crowded, Elder, Vanderhoven and Le Prieur found a table near the door, ordered dinner and fell to talking shop.

Just outside in the lobby, an elderly Artillery sergeant, who wore the ribbons of the Mons Star and several other World War decorations, was suddenly moved to song.

"Sitting in the 'Ouse of Commons
Myking laws to put down crime,
While the wictim of 'is pash-shuns
Walks the streets without a ny-y-yme ..."

"Gosh, there's an old song!" grinned Elder. "I remember the first time I ever heard it. — It was one night in Liverpool, during the last war."

"Ach, the last war!" Captain Vanderhoven put down his soup spoon and shuddered. "— Will we ever, ever, ever be able to say '*the last*

116

war' and mean it as the last war for all time —
instead of merely the one before this?"

"If you didn't think so — if you weren't
sure of it — you wouldn't be here now!" said
Elder.

Captain Le Prieur nodded and looked
down at the scarlet Cross of Lorraine on the
France Libre badge pinned to his right breast.
"We can all be sure. — Because there is a God!"
he murmured, confidently.

"That I know!" said the Dutchman. "He is
a kind God, a just God!" He shuddered again
and closed his eyes. "I know He will forgive me
for that moment when I-I-almost cursed Him!"

"— Oh, — What moment was that, Van?"

Captain Vanderhoven's eyes were still
closed as he replied. "That moment," he said
slowly, "the exact moment, was thirty-one
minutes past one in the afternoon. — The
afternoon of May fourteenth, Nineteen hundred
-and-forty. — In Rotterdam …"

"Oh?"

"Yes." He paused for some time before
resuming. "I — I am sorry that neither of you
gentlemen ever met my wife. She was a good
woman. We were happy, so very happy, for all

the nine years we had each other. And then, one day, she told me that we were to be — happier still! Our prayers had been answered!

"Well, I had orders for Java, but I left with a light heart. Her health was good, and I knew that I would be back in time. In Batavia, her letters were waiting for me, happy letters, because all was going fine. We called at four or five ports along the coast, picked up our rubber and started home. At Aden there were more letters. Hers were as gay as ever, but there was one from her mother which seemed worried. — Worried about my wife. — Worried that the Germans might come into Holland. Of this war talk, I was not troubled. 'It is talk', I said, 'just talk, more talk!.' But of my wife, I was troubled greatly. Somehow, I felt, I knew, that I must get home to her quickly. And so, going up the Red Sea, I am always at the speaking tube, asking Mr. Veidt, my engineer, to squeeze another knot out of her. And at Suez there is some question about our Canal tolls, but I sign the chit without wasting time to argue.

"We are well into the Mediterranean when we hear that the Germans are on the move. I send a wireless to my owners asking for orders.

— Should I put into Gibraltar, or some English port? The answer is *'Proceed to Rotterdam.'* I know, now, it was the Fifth Column. The Germans wanted that shipload of rubber! But at that time, I am relieved, because I must get to Rotterdam — to my wife!

"And so finally we are there. We dock below the *Schiedamschedykstraat* and no sooner are we made fast than I rush ashore, jump into a tram-car and start for my home. The people in the tram-car all are saying that the Germans are in the suburbs, but they are not excited. Some say we can defend the city; Others say we will accept a *'peaceful* occupation,' 'a *protective* occupation.' But the wattman calls back from the platform that on his previous trip he has heard firing, and seen three hundred bombers landing in the fields just east of the city. But — of this I do not worry. I worry of my wife …

"So I get down from the tram at the *Zeelandstraat.* I walk, I run, to my house, it is at *Zeelandstraat* Number Twenty-four. Outside it, I see the little black Opel car of Doctor Ziemer, and leaning against a tree is a bicycle — a woman's bicycle. There is a white wicker basket on the luggage rack behind the saddle, and so I recognize it as the bicycle of Mrs. Rhenst, she is the neighborhood midwife.

"My heart stops, because it is a month too early, but — I go in. There is no one around. I smell chloroform. Standing in the hall outside the bedroom door, I see the little carved oak cradle that for three hundred years all Vanderhovens have lain in. Then the bedroom door opens and out comes Doctor Ziemer. He has got his coat off and his sleeves are rolled up. And he — yes, he is *smiling!*

"'Why, Captain!,' he says, 'Welcome home! You're just in time, old boy! Ha, ha! Yes, yes, yes! For a while we were worried, but now everything is doing fine!'

"I try to push past him into the bedroom, but this he will not permit. 'No, no, old boy — not yet, not yet!,' he says to me. 'Go outside on the *straat*, smoke one cigar, and by the time you have finished, we will have good news for you!'

"'Doctor!,' I cry, grasping him of the hand. 'You are not having me on, Doctor? — Everything is really all right? — You are not pulling my leg, Doctor?'

"'No, on my word of honor! Go to the outside and smoke a cigar! And save one for me, old boy!'"

Captain Vanderhoven paused, raised his glass to his lips and then put it down without drinking.

"Just then," he said, "Just then ... we both hear it! It is a little sound — *mew!* — like a kitten! Doctor Ziemer slaps me on the back and runs in at the bedroom door. 'See you in a minute-Papa!' he hollers me ...

"And so I go outside on the *Zeelandstraat*, which has a little canal flowing along beside. I am smoking my cigar and feeling so very happy, and when the policeman comes along on his bicycle I give him also a cigar. It is a very good cigar which comes from Sumatra. The *gendarme* smells it and says me, 'Oh, thank you, Captain! I cannot smoke it now, but I will put it in my helmet and smoke it later.'

"'Helmet?' I say. 'Oh, I did not until this now moment notice that you were wearing a helmet. — Why are you wearing this helmet? It must be damned uncomfortable!'

"'It is *Goddverdampt* uncomfortable,' he says me. 'I am only wearing it until after the

Alert is called off, which will be at one-thirty precisely. — In fact,' he says me, looking at his watch, 'if we walk out here on this little bridge spanning the canal over, we can see the Konigsbrug, where pretty soon the red rocket will be shot up. The red rocket will end the what-you-may-call-it-the *ultimatum*. When the Germans see the red rocket, they will not be to bomb us!'

"So I walk out on the little bridge spanning the canal over, and I look toward the Konigsbrug and I look toward my watch and — and I look toward my home. And then I look up toward Heaven and I pray to God Almighty to call up the red rocket — the red rocket! And — sure enough! — a red rocket squirts up, *shriff-f-f!* from the Konigsbrug. Another one comes up from the Willembrug. *Shriff-f-f!*

"So I say to the policeman, 'You can congratulate me, officer! By, this time I am certainly a father!' And I hand him another cigar.

"The policeman bows politely and takes off again his helmet, to put therein my second Sumatra cigar. And suddenly there is a noise and he is standing there, politely, but —

without a head. He topples over, because his head is gone. So is his helmet. — And then — so is the bridge! And I — I am lying there beside the canal, looking at my home and all around is a stinking yellow smoke. But in it I can smell a trace of chloroform. And — and so I get up! ...

"— But — but why did I bother to get up? — Why?" Captain Vanderhoven's voice was tense, hoarse. "Why did I bother to get up? ..."

"Steady, Van! Come! Tell us what, happened!"

"Why — my heart had been killed! Where had been my home was only — nothing! Nothing! Nothing! — Just a hole in der groundt, with smoke and a bad smell coming oudt! I walk towards it and suddenly I stumble over something on the sidewalk. It is the little carved oak cradle that for three hundred years all the Vanderhovens have lain in. But now, but now, it is filled with ... Ach, God!"

Elder leaned across the table and gripped him by the shoulder. "All right, Van! " he said. "So that was that! So you went back down to the *Schiedamschedykstraat*, didn't you, and took your ship across to England? — In spite of hell?"

"Why, yes," said Captain Vanderhoven, evenly. "Why yes — as a matter of fact, I did. — The trams weren't running because, you see, the Stukas were overhead and ... well, and so I rode down to the harbor on the midwife's bicycle. Most of the ships in the port were burning, but for some reason, mine was not. For some reason, I got her over to England. For some reason, I've got her here. For some reason, I'll get her to Murmansk. — And what is that reason? — Ask God!"

15

SILHOUETTED against the dawn-red-
dened sky, the Union Jack of the
British Empire stirred languidly on its
staff above Citadel Hill. The sun climbed
higher, dispelling the blanket of mist which in
the night had shrouded the ships in the harbor.
On board these ships, thousands of men were
toiling feverishly, as indeed they had toiled for
hours. From the stokeholds of ancient Clyde-
built coalburners came the thump of slice bars,
the scrape of shovels on steel plates and the

clang of furnace doors. In oil-fired stokeholds, jets of flame spurted from the nozzles and then, as the fuel vaporized, fell to roaring like giant blowtorches. The decks of motorships throbbed and trembled under foot as the high-compression Diesels went rumbling into action. Here and there along the tensely-waiting ranks, plumes of steam shot hissing from main exhausts. Windlasses *clunk-clunked!* as scope in the chains was shortened and the vessels were brought up directly over their anchors, ready to put to sea.

"It kind of makes you think of a big city getting set for a busy day," observed Captain Elder, on the bridge of the *Merchant Mariner*.

"Yes, sir," agreed Cadet Parker. He swung up his binoculars and trained them upon the Naval anchorage. "Look there, sir! The minesweepers are putting out, now, and —yes, there go the destroyers!"

Elder levelled his glasses. "The cruiser's weighing anchor, too," he announced. "Oh! Good morning, pilot!"

"Morning, sir! Fine day to start your trip."

"— Yes," Elder consulted his watch. "— And it won't be long, now!"

At six o'clock precisely, the S.S. *Cortez*, Admiral Hartridge's commander ship, broke out her identifying pennants and swept majestically toward the open sea. Sixty seconds later, a stackless Norwegian motorship plowed down the fairway, to be followed, a minute later, by a rusty and decrepit three-thousand tonner flying the blue-and-white ensign of Greece.

Elder considered her pityingly and shook his head. "That's the *Thalassa*," he said. "Poor old Nick Papodoulos! — Wife and kids starving to death in Piraeus and him setting out on this picnic in that God-awful tub!"

"I hear she's loaded to the guards with TNT," said the pilot.

"Yes, and I'm glad to see she's Number Seventy, said Elder, shrugging. "That means she won't be near us, anyway."

"They always put the hot ones in the outside positions," the pilot explained. "— Then, if they get hit, they don't blow up the whole bloody convoy."

Ship after ship got under way. At 6:41 came the *Merchant Mariner's* turn. Her anchors came up, and with the deck hoses sluicing the

Halifax mud from them, she swung into line and joined the procession seaward.

"What's that they're saying, up there at the Signal Station, Parker?"

The cadet scanned the hoist of bright-colored flags through his glasses. "They're signalling 'Good Luck,' sir."

Six Catalinas and two big four-motored Coronados went roaring past on the water, lifted out of their own spray and soared off to sea, carrying depth bombs under their wings.

Proceeding in line ahead, the great ocean caravan slid through the harbor mouth and bore northeastward toward the point of rendezvous. Ahead of it was the mine-sweeper fringe; then came the destroyers, flotilla leaders and a light cruiser, while more destroyers coursed back and forth upon the flanks.

The blinker lamp on the *Cortez* was flashing, now. "They're starting to form up," said the pilot. A destroyer came back along the line, its loud speaker calling out raucously. *"Watch your numbers, please! Watch your numbers, please! Take up your position three hundred yards from the ships fore-and-aft and abeam."*

"Well, now you can take over, Captain," said the pilot. "From here on, it's your show."

The *Merchant Mariner* steamed in among the ships of the gathering convoy and took her place behind Number Forty-eight; Number Fifty-seven was not yet in position. As the vessels moved slowly ahead, with bare steerage way, motorboats plied from one to another of them, picking up the pilots.

Number Fifty-seven drew up on the port quarter, coming fast. "Guess he doesn't want to be late for school," said the pilot. "— Still, he'd better ... Say! What the hell's the matter with him? Look out, Captain! He's taking a sheer straight for us!"

"Full right!" Elder shouted to the helmsman, at the same time shoving the telegraph to FULL AHEAD. The *Merchant Mariner* swung out of line as the other ship regained control and headed back toward its station.

"Phew! That was a close one, Captain! Nice work!"

"M'mph!" said Elder. "Guess that fellow's steering gear must've jammed."

"The Commander Ship is making our number, Sir," said Parker. *"Number Fifty-eight"* he read the blinker flashes, *"Number Fifty-eight ... You ... are ... out ... of ... position ... Regain ... immediately."*

"— Hunh? — What's that? — Why, the blethering old goat!" Elder stormed. "— Is it my fault I'm out of line? What the hell does he mean, bawling me out before the whole convoy? I've got a mind to signal him to go take a good, brisk run for himself! Yunh! — A run around right end!"

The pilot grinned. "They say old Hartridge is a proper tough bloke! A chap was telling me about one time when ... Oh! Here comes my boat alongside." He extended his hand. "Well, Captain, I wish you good luck, fair weather and a safe return!"

When the convoy was finally in formation, its main body made a rectangle whose area covered nearly four square miles. *"Course ... sixty-two ... degrees ... Speed ... nine ... knots ... Proceed."* Parker read the flashes from the *Cortez*. The seventy-three vessels moved ahead as one. The great fleet looked like a city which in some miraculous fashion had broken loose from terra firma and gone adventuring on the sea.

"Jeece, some sight!" said Stanislawski. He and his companions were sprawled in the sun on the tarpaulin cover of Number Four hatch. On the well-deck all around them were wingless Lockheed bombers.

"Some sight is right! Say — how much dough would you guess all these ships and cargoes is worth?

"How much? Hell, there *ain't* that much!"

"No, you wouldn't think so, would you? And yet, all this we're looking at ain't a drop in the bucket, compared to what the whole war's costing!"

"Yair — and what's the sense of it?" said a sailor. "— That's what I wanta know!"

"That's what everybody wants to know, except Hitler. The only thing he don't know is that he's crazy!"

"Yair, sure! — But what I wanta know is, what's it all about? — I mean, as far as ordinary guys like us is concerned?"

"Hell!" said Larson, gruffly, shoving a charge of Copenhagen snuff into his cheek, "—

You vant to know vat it's all about, do you?
Vell, I guess you vass neffer in the Axis ports and
seen how them poor people liff! — I guess you
do not know about Norway, where the people
— my people — are slafes! But for Chrisakes,
you dope — dit'nt you neffer hear about the
Four Freedoms?"

"— Four Freedoms? — You mean them
four, now, pernts that President Roosevelt made
that speech about? — Well, yair, I heard him on
the radio, but I guess I've — I've kinda forgot
exactly what they was."

"Den you should be ashamedt of yourself!
— But neffer mind, neffer mind! ... Vait! — I
vill make it all clear to you!"

Larson rose to his feet. His eyes were
bright and his nostrils dilated. Obviously, he
was moved by a deep, a religious, an all-
consuming fervor ...

"Stant up, you!"

With a wink to the crowd, the other
obeyed and stood there, grinning.

"Vell, how do you feel?"

"Feel? Me? Oh, I feel swell! — But
shucks, Larson — I thought you was going to..."

Suddenly the carpenter's horny hands shot out and gripped him by the throat. — Gripped it, squeezed it, clamped upon it, until the membranous walls of the windpipe met and stuck together. The fellow emitted a single hoarse gurgle and then struggled futilely, his eyes and tongue protruding.

The muscles of Larson's forearms stood out like grape vines as he clamped harder and harder. He chuckled through his scraggly mustache. "Vell! Now ... now ... now you are liffing in an Axis country! It's a great life ... ain't it? Oh, it's luffly! Poy, oh poy, oh poy — how you are enchoying yourself! You got a strong man, a dictator, a *Führer*, a *Duce* and he is in charge of everyt'ing! He tells you vat to think! He tells you vat to do! He giffs you vateffer you need — except for one thing! ... Vell, vat iss that one thing?" Suddenly Larson relaxed his grip, stepped back a pace and stood with hands dramatically upraised. "— Ah! Ah-h-h! Now you can breathe! Now, you are free! Now, you are in a democracy! Now, you can fill your lungs vit the good air that God made for us all! — Vell! ..." He turned and spread his arms toward the Stars and Stripes which fluttered at the stern. "— Vell! You asked vat we are fighting for! — Now, I — I guess you know, maybe!"

Like the rest of them, Jeff Caldwell, the Negro pantryman, was deeply impressed by this practical demonstration of the comparative values of life under totalitarianism and democracy. But still, something seemed to be troubling him. He sat down beside Stanislawski and spoke confidentially.

"The only thing Ah can't figure out is where us colored folks is going to get anything from this war. — Tell me, Stan — what chance has a boy like me got, in a democracy or in any other place?"

"— What chance have you got? — In America? Why hell, Jeff — what chance did Joe Louis have? — Only enough chance to make eighty-three million bucks for himself, cash money!"

"M'm, yes ... but Ah ain't got a left like Joe!"

"Awright, awright, and so what? — How about Rochester? There's a colored boy he ain't even as strong as you are, but he pulls down ten thousand smackers a week for talkin' five minutes over the radio and five hundred grand every time he acts in a picture!"

"Fahve hunnerd grand? — Unh-*unh*! Oh, boy! Ain't dat sumpin!"

"You're dam tootin' it's somethin'! But say, lissen, Jeff! — Get this! Now, here's exackly what you and I are gonta do! As soon as we win this war, see, we'll go out to Hollywood and crash the movies. The way I figure it, what's this guy Victor Mature got that I haven't got? — Yair — and what's this colored guy Rochester got that you haven't got?"

"Um, well — he's got fahve hunnerd grand!"

"Sure! Sure! — But how'd he get it? Why, he got it simply by sayin', '*Hello, Mistah Benny — this is Rochester,*' that's how he got it! Jeff, you just come along to Hollywood with me and you'n I'll show them guys some talent! — How about it, kid?"

"— Say! You don't really mean it, Stan?"

"Sure I really mean it! I'll start coachin' you right now, so's you'll be all set to knock 'em stiff as soon as we get there! C'mon, now — let's hear you say '*Hello, Mistah Benny — this is Rochester*'"

"Aw, shucks!" Jeff simpered in embarrassment and twisted at a button of his white jacket. "Ah — Ah — Ah . . . Aw, shucks!"

"Oh, come on, now — don't be noivous! There ain't nobody gonta bite you!"

"Well (tish-hish!) — er, er — *Hello, Mistah Benny — this is Rochester!*"

"At-a-boy! Say, that's swell! — The only thing, Jeff, you want to make it a little hoarser, like you'd swallered a handful of gravel or something. — Now, just gimme it again ..."

"Er — *Hello, Mistah Benny — this is Rochester! — How's that, hunh?"*

"Too fast! — Just a little too fast! But just you keep on rehearsing, Jeff — it'll come to you all of a sudden. Yes, sir! By the time this war's over, I guarantee you'll be saying it poifect!"

With the light of a new-found ambition kindled in his eye, Jefferson Caldwell moved happily toward the pantry, repeating his lines and trying to sound as though he had swallowed a handful of gravel.

16

L ATE that night, Captain Elder was in his cabin, once more studying his convoy orders. Mr. Rossi stuck his head in at the door.

"Oh, hello there, Joe! — Come on in and we'll go over this stuff together. But first, just yell down to Jeff to shoot us up some sandwiches and beer, will you?"

"Okay," said Mr. Rossi. "But why don't you use that phone, right there at your elbow?"

"Phone? Oh, sure! Gosh, Joe, it's funny, but I can't seem to get used to all the modern trimmings on this ship! — As a matter of fact, I sometimes think it's all a little screwy. H'm, let's see, now ... *Seven* ... that's the pantry number. Hello!"

"*Hello, Mistah Benny — this is Rochester!*" came a hoarse but sleepy voice.

"— Hunh? — Rochester? — I don't want Rochester and I don't want Syracuse! I want the pantry and ... Unh! Oh! — Say, what the hell's the matter with you, Jeff — been hitting that lemon extract again? — Bring up four hams-on-rye and two bottles of beer, and make it snappy!"

17

AT nightfall, each ship displayed a single tiny light, so shielded as to be visible only from dead astern. With their guidance, and the light of the quarter moon, maintaining the formation presented no great difficulty. From time to time a destroyer passed up and down the lanes, looking for lights like an air raid warden enforcing a blackout. Once it ran alongside the ship behind the *Merchant Mariner.* *"Tanker, ahoy-y-y!"* its loudspeaker bawled, *"You've got a Porthole*

uncovered aft. Fix it at once or we'll machine gun it!"

"Gee!" said Cadet Parker, "That fellow sounds as though he meant business!"

"Yes," chuckled Mr. Rossi. "— I hate to think what would happen if he pulled that stuff on the Old Man, though!"

For a while the pair stood silent, looking out at the great, dark forms that moved so majestically through the night and at the glowing white patches in the churned-up water. At length, Rossi stirred.

"You know, since this morning, I bet I've heard twenty guys say that this convoy looks like a city. — And it does, by God! It kind of — oh, I dunno! — it kind of makes me feel at home. — Or maybe it makes me homesick!"

"Well, not me!" said Parker. "Of course, I don't know much about cities, but gosh! I do know I'd hate to live in one."

"Well, that's where you and I are different, John. — Me ... why, I guess I'd just go nuts, if I was cooped up in some little town."

"But you wouldn't be cooped up in a little town, Joe! The smaller the town, the freer you are. Now, you take my home town, Glorietta,

Kansas. You can drive through it in two minutes, sure — but you'll drive for five hours before you strike another town. — If it's freedom you want, you sure can get plenty of it out in that country!"

"But — but what's out there? All that land, I mean! — Is it woods or swamps or mountains or what?"

"It's prairies. It's corn-fields. — It's wheat-fields. — It's pastures. Thousands and thousands and thousands of square miles of them! Why, that country's as big as the sea, Joe! Yes, and when the wind blows through the grass and the crops, they move just like the waves of the sea."

"Well, I'll be damned!" said Mr. Rossi, wonderingly. "I — I really never thought it would be anything like that! Of course, I was born down on Rivington Street and — well, I guess there must be a whole lot more to America than I imagined!"

"You bet there is, and all of it's pretty good!" Cadet Parker was silent for a moment. "Yes, it's … pretty good! Well, I guess I'll go down and — and try to write a letter. Good night, Joe!"

"Good night, Johnny!"

As he was passing the radio room, Parker decided to stop in a moment for a chat and a smoke with Sparks. He found the operator, a tall, dark chap of about his own age, twiddling with his dials.

"Hi, Sparks! Anything coming over?"

"Not much. I'm just trying to clear up this German station. — I think it's Hamburg. — The guy's speaking English. — Wait — no — yes — here it is!"

He shoved an extra headset to Parker, who took off his cap and adjusted it over his ears.

"This is Hamburg calling," came a voice with that peculiar, coldly-insolent head-waiter intonation characteristic of all German propaganda broadcasters. "This is Hamburg, calling — calling to all the sailors of the Allied ships at sea. — Or perhaps I should say, *all those ships which have not yet been sunk!* Oh, yes, you poor fellows, you poor sailors — we are sinking so many, so many, so ... many! Of course, your Jewish masters, those dear friends of Churchill and Roosevelt, those international bankers who own the ships — they do not tell you the truth!

Ha, ha! — Of course they don't! — Why should they? — They have insured their ships for five or six times their real value and when one is sunk, it is a bit of good luck for them! But what about you, you poor, brave but deluded sailors? — Why, you get drowned, like so many rats! And what happens to your wives and children, then? — Why, naturally, to keep from starving, they take in the washing, they scrub the floors, they wait at the table; they are the servants, the slaves, the mistresses, even, of the fat, war-mongering bloodsuckers who murdered — *you!*"

Parker chuckled and turned to wink at Sparks. But the fellow appeared to be spellbound. His face was pale and his hand trembled as he raised it to adjust the dial.

"But now, my dear sailors, it is time that you knew the truth!" the voice continued. "— The truth about how many of your ships are being sunk! And because each ship that sinks is the coffin of many brave sailors, we think it only fitting that we count each ship with a chime of the death knell. — How many have been sunk this week? — Count the chimes! Count them! *Count!*" There was an instant of silence; then

143

"BONG!" came the solemn, eerie note of a bell. "*BONG! . . . BONG . . . BONG! . . . .*"

"Aw, BONG! to you!" laughed Parker, snatching off his earphones. "Why, if that Nazi heel ever ..."

"Sh-h! Sh-h!" Sparks held up his trembling, cigarette-stained hand. "*Seven ... Eight ... Nine ... Ten ... Eleven ... Twelve ...*"

Abruptly, Parker reached over and spun the dial off the tuning. "Sparks!" he cried, "Sparks! For the love of Mike, kid, snap out of it!"

"Okay, okay! But ... holy smoke, Johnny! Do you believe it's true!"

"Sure, I believe it's true! — Germans cannot tell a lie! Didn't you ever hear the story about Hitler and the cherry tree?"

"No, no — I mean — all kidding aside! This is no matter for kidding, Johnny!"

"Sure, it isn't! If you don't like kidding, don't listen to Germany!" said Parker, reaching for his cap. He yawned. "— Well, now I guess I'll mosey on down and try to write a letter. G'night, Sparks! — Better not go out on deck in the dark! — The boogey man'll ketch you if you don't watch out!"

18

ONE Round Kid Ahearn, Texas Fitch and Hyman Goldberg, three gallant bluejackets of the United States Navy, were eating supper with the second sitting of the ship's civilian crew. They had scupped up the soup and now the meat course was brought to the table.

"Wow!" exclaimed Ahearn, his battered face lighting up joyfully. "Roast sugar-cured Virginia ham! — Wit' cloves! — Wit' gravy!

— Wit' candied sweet pertaters! Wow! — Lemme at it!"

"Now wait, wai-i-i-t, just a minute!" Goldberg restrained him. "— If you want me to handle you when the war's over, ya gotta watch your weight, Kid! — What I mean, you're supposed to be a middleweight, ain'tcha? — You're supposed to weigh a mere a hunnerd and sixty pounds, ain'tcha? Well — do you wanta eat your way up into the heavyweight class and git ya block knocked off? Do ya wanta be 'One Round' Ahearn all your life? Wouldn'tcha like to see what it feels like to stay two rounds, fer a change?"

"Aw, shucks, Hymie — I only weigh a hunnerd and seventy-t'ree and I can train down in no time! — What's thoiteen pounds?"

"Thoiteen pounds ain't dandruff!" said Goldberg. "You just foller my example and go easy on the chow, that's all!" He helped himself to a sweet potato and took no ham at all.

"Aw, jeece, Hymie!" said Kid Ahearn, plaintively. "I got an appetite on me I could choke a Wolf wit'!"

"Well, say — you gents shore are missing something!" declared Texas Fitch, drawlingly.

He heaped his plate and then proceeded to smother the pile of fodder with black pepper, red pepper, ketchup, piccalilli, horseradish, mustard, tabasco, chili and Worcestershire. "Oh, Mammy!" he breathed, ecstatically, masticating a fork-load. 'This shore is food! Yes, suh-h-h! It takes me back down deep in the heart of Texas!"

"Heart? Phew! Heartburn, ya mean!" said Stanislawski. "Don'tcha want me to spray you wit' a fire extinguisher, Tex?"

"Don't bother! But say — do you Merchant Marine guys always eat as fancy as this?"

"— Fancy? — You call this fancy? Why, shucks — Mike Golubeff, the cook, don't dare trot out his usual fancy stuff on account he's afraid you Navy guys might get seasick."

Texas Fitch helped himself to another sweet potato, doused it with tabasco sauce and consumed it without a flicker.

"Hey, Cowboy — when you're all finished settin' fire to your liver, you might pass that platter down this way!" said little Smitty, hungrily. "Ya know, it'll really be a change to eat some of this plain, simple chow, after all them rich, de luxe Automat dishes Mike usually makes."

"Here y'are, Smitty!"

"Keep it in circulation!"

"Next!"

"Coming up!"

Hyman Goldberg watched as they helped themselves to the thick, pink, crispy-edged, clove-studded slices. He watched as they harpooned the sugar-candied yams and flooded them with rich, brown gravy. He watched — and watching, licked his lips. Presently, he stretched and yawned. "Oh, ho, hum!" he said, shrugging with elaborate indifference. "Hey, Tex — if there's any more of that *gefulte*-fish left, you might pass it down here."

"— Hunh? Ger-whatta fish? — You mean this ham, Hymie?"

"— Ham? Ham, he says! — What ham?" Hastily, Goldberg shovelled four slices onto his plate. "Ham, phooey!" he scoffed. "— If you dopes down in Texas have got funny names for things, is it my fault?"

"Aw, hey, now, jeece, Hymie!" Kid Ahearn pleaded. "Won'tcha please, please,

please lemme have just a little teeny, weeny, itsy bit?"

Hyman Goldberg rolled his eyes toward heaven. "As God is my witness, I'd like to, Kid!" he answered, righteously. "But — no! — I mustn't! I can't! I won't! I'll never forget my duties as your manager! And besides — looka, Kid — there ain't any more!"

ACTION IN THE NORTH ATLANTIC

19

A CATALINA came droning through the late northern twilight, circled the convoy for some minutes and then headed back into the east.

"Looks like he brought a report from up ahead," said Mr. Rossi.

"Yes — fog, probably," agreed Captain Elder. "This month's North Atlantic Pilot Chart shows a Thirty per cent fog area from Cape Race clear out to Forty-three West."

From the van of the convoy came the throaty hoot of the *Cortez's* whistle as she signalled for attention. Her Aldis lamp commenced blinking. "'All ... ships!'" Rossi read. "*Dense fog ... reported ... twenty ... miles ... ahead ... Have ... spars ... in ... readiness ... for ... streaming! ...*'"

"M'mph!" grunted Elder. "Spars, eh? Well, it looks like we're in for a pleasant evening! Look there, Joe — those squareheads on Number Forty-eight are getting all set!"

The mate peered ahead at the Norwegian vessel, across whose poop a group of men were lugging a heavy wooden spar.

"Well, ours is already rigged," he said. "It's not just a plain spar, either! I've got a big square of white canvas laced onto it so's it'll float along behind. It looks like a dance-floor! If those chumps back there in Number Sixty-eight can't see it ... Well!" Mr. Rossi doubled his right fist and shot it, SMACK! into his left palm. "— Well, when we get ashore in Murmansk, I'll-I'll ..."

"Now, now, t'st, t'st, t'st, Mr. Rossi!"

"Okay! Okay, sir! I'll just go aft and make sure the bosun and Blair have got the bridle rigged right."

The pink flush in the sky cooled to purple; the purple deepened and became slate gray. The vessels in the convoy's ranks faded from sharp, clean silhouettes to vague, murky shapes which plodded slowly toward the looming wall of utter darkness which was the fog.

Just before she reached it, the *Cortez* flashed a signal. "*Reduce ... speed ... to ... Seven ... Knots ... Stream ... spars ...*" Then there was a pause, punctuated by hesitant flickerings, as though whoever was dictating to the signaller could not make up his mind.

"H'mph! Looks like the old goat's trying to decide whether he wants to say Ker-hapf or Ker-hem! — Or maybe he's getting ready to chase himself around right end!" But just then the blinker resumed its flashing. "*Good night ... and ... good luck ... signed ... Hartridge*" it read.

"Oh!" said Elder. "Oh! That's — different!" He raised his hand toward the *Cortez* in a friendly gesture. "Good night and good luck to you, Admiral!" he murmured.

The great ship plunged into the fog, and was gone.

20

"GOD! This is a bad one! Elder grunted.

Mr. Rossi nodded, the movement dislodging drops of water from his chin, his nose and the brim of his oilskin sou'wester. "I'll say!" he agreed. "Damned stuff's pretty near solid!"

"How many men have you got for'ard?"

"Four, on the foc'sle head. I've got 'em looking straight down at the water. — No use their trying to see anything ahead!"

"How's that Norwegian's spar working?"

"All right, so far. We pretty near ran over it, once, but ..."

A bell clanged on the foc'sle head and a fog-muffled voice shouted, "*Spa-a-ar ahead!*"

"Ring 'er down!" ordered Elder.

Rossi shoved the telegraph to DEAD SLOW.

"I hope to God that tanker in back of us doesn't chew our spar off!" said Elder, anxiously peering aft. But it was like looking into a dark closet.

"Captain! ... There!" a shout came from the starboard bridge lookout. "— Something white — a spar! Right here on the beam!"

"Ten left!" Elder barked to the man at the wheel. He ran out into the wing and looked over the side. There, sure enough, he saw a track of white foam — heard a dull thump-thumping as the trailing spar dragged against the *Merchant Mariner's* plates. Slowly, slowly, the ship answered her helm; the thumping ceased, the white track faded and then was swallowed by the murk.

"Whew!" said Elder. "This is worse than playing blind man's buff inside a cow! If we'd slowed down any more, or stopped, we'd have had that tanker astern of us climbing aboard over our taffrail!"

"We would, if he's still back there!" said Mr. Rossi, grimly.

The bosun appeared upon the bridge. "Our spar's gone, sir!" he reported. "Somebody bit the line off lessn' fifty yards astern of us. We're rigging another."

"Who was it — could you see?"

"No, sir, but it wasn't the tanker."

"M'mph! M' mph! Well, it's a cinch the whole convoy's in a mess, by now. — Couldn't help but be!"

And so, for hour after hour, they stood their unavailing vigil. Always, they were oppressed by the consciousness of unseen vessels all around them. Once, somewhere away to port, they heard the rending crunch of steel against steel, hoarse shouts and the sound of thrashing water. Again, a vessel drew abeam of them, so close that for a single awful instant they could see the white faces of the men on her bridge and feel the hot breath from her funnel; then she slid away from them and vanished like a ghost-ship in the fog.

"Br-rh!" shuddered Mr. Rossi. "Johnny Parker's right! — Give me the wide-open spaces of Kansas!"

For a long while they were silent, straining their eyes and their ears; then, "Look up there," said Elder, pointing skyward. "It's getting light; the dawn's leaking through."

"Yes, thank God!" said Rossi. "— And it shows that this fog can't go up so very high. Maybe they can use planes to get us herded back together."

The fog ahead of them turned gray, then white, then pink. Suddenly, lo, they were out in the clear! Before them, black against the rising sun, were ships of the scattered convoy. Even as they looked, more and more of them came plowing out of the fog.

"Well, they've pretty badly scrambled but not as badly as I expected," said Elder.

"There's the *Cortez* way over there to port. She's stopped to let us form up on her."

"Yes, and there's the cruiser. M'm, now, let's see — can you make out any of these fellows' numbers? That's the old *Thalassa*, up ahead; I can recognize her by that ..."

"God!"

Where the *Thalassa* had been, there reared a towering pillar of fire and smoke. A gust, a gale, a tornado swept across the water — a mighty, invisible force which buffetted the *Merchant Mariner*, rocked her, wrenched her, and caused her to quiver and tremble. Then came a roar such as mortal ear had never heard before. For miles around, white splashes leaped and danced on the surface of the sea as fragments of men and metal came raining down upon it. For minutes, it seemed, this fearful shower continued. Elder sickened as he watched it. The smoke cloud rolled itself into a big, greasy ball and drifted lazily down the wind. Of the *Thalassa*, there remained no slightest trace. Nothing. Nothing.

Elder groaned. "Poor Nick Papodoulos!"

Off to starboard, a ship's whistle hooted frenziedly; then came two muffled explosions and she heeled over on her side.

"Periscope! Dead Astern!" bawled one of the *Merchant Mariner's* lookouts.

"Periscope! Port Beam!" cried another.

Simultaneously, the *Merchant Mariner's* four inch gun let go with an ear-splitting WHAM! and the .50 calibres behind the bridge

159

snarled as though ripping the air asunder. Elder could see the bullets lashing the water to foam. In the midst of the foam there jutted something which looked like a drain pipe. Suddenly, the drain pipe snapped off short and toppled into the water.

From somewhere ahead came the sound of heavy firing and the muffled booming of depth bombs. A plane shot away from the cruiser's catapult, and was followed by another. Elder saw a destroyer plunging toward him; suddenly, she seemed to rear up backwards, her bow enveloped in smoke. When the smoke cleared, her bow was under water and her stern thrust high in the air, the propellers lashing futilely. For a moment she hung poised and then nose-dived out of sight.

"Hell!" cried Rossi, "There's subs all around! It's lousy with 'em!"

"Yunh! We've been jumped by a whole bloody pack! We've got to get out of here!" He snatched up the Engine Room telephone. "Give 'er everything she's got! Everything! Understand me, Mister?

A white torpedo trail came streaking from dead ahead, directly toward the *Merchant*

Mariner's bow. Elder shouldered the helmsman away from the wheel and grasped it himself. Obviously, if he kept the ship on her course, the torpedo would meet her squarely. If he swung her out of line, the impact would be somewhere on the side. It was a supreme test of seamanship — a test involving split second judgment and unexampled skill. Elder hunched his shoulders, gripped the wheel tighter and — grinned!

Just as a direct, head-on hit appeared inevitable, he eased her a trifle to the right, then eased her a trifle more. As the torpedo plunged into the first bow wave, he jammed on full left rudder. The tin fish was shoved sideways by the surging, tumbling bow wave like a beetle in a gutter torrent. It streaked harmlessly along the *Merchant Mariner's* entire length, a scant four feet away.

A breathless cheer went up, followed by cries of "Nice work, Captain!" "At-a-boy, sir!" and "That's dodging 'em, Skipper!"

"M'mph!" Elder grunted, more than a little pleased with himself. "Well, it was a damned neat job, at that!"

He swung the ship due north and relinquished the wheel to the quartermaster.

"Hold her as she bears," he ordered.

The *Cortez*, her four guns blazing, was signalling *"Disperse ... Disperse ... Disperse ..."* The command was superfluous, for the ships of the convoy were scattering in all directions. But even when the *Merchant Mariner* was out of sight of the last of them, Elder could still hear the dull rumble, the troubled mutter, of gun fire below the southern horizon.

All through the rest of that tragic day, the *Merchant Mariner* plied her northward course. Early in the evening, Sparks emerged from the radio room and moved weakly toward a ventilator, against which he leaned, for support. His face was ashen, his lips twitched and his nails were bitten to the quick. Evidently, the night of fog and the morning of battle had shaken him badly.

For a while he stood there, gazing dully out upon the sunset-reddened sea. Then, suddenly, he stiffened. "Say!" he gasped, "We're heading North! What are we heading North for?"

Impulsively, blindly, he made for the bridge ladder and ascended it.

"Mr. Rossi!" he blurted. "Is the Captain here?"

"He's there in the chart room. What's the matter, Sparks — got a message for him?"

"No, I ... Oh, Captain! Captain!" As Elder came out of the door, Sparks ran forward and seized him by the hand. "We're — we're heading North! North, sir! *North!*"

"Why, sure we're heading North! Say ... what the hell's the matter with you, Sparks! — Let go of my hand!"

"But — but we've lost the convoy! We've lost the escort! If we try to make it alone, it'll — it'll be suicide! Aren't you going to put back, Captain?"

"Put back? Of course I'm not going to put back! But one more yip out of you, Mister, and I'll put you in irons!"

"But Captain — oh, please, please! For the love of God, Captain!" Sparks voice cracked shrilly. "Put back while there's time! — Put back while ..."

SOCK!

Sparks went down like an empty sack and lay there, moaning thinly.

"Okay, Joe!" Elder nodded his approval. "For once in your life, you uncorked it on the right guy. Some day, I bet this lad will thank you for it! Yes, indeed! It'll make a man of him, or I miss my guess!"

"Um!" said Mr. Rossi, "Um! I wish these damn knuckles could get a chance to heal up!"

"Hey, Johnny!" Elder called to Parker, "— Help Sparks down to his room and put him to bed, will you? — Tell the assistant operator to stay on the job till he's feeling better."

"Bed?" said Rossi, endeavoring unsuccessfully to stifle a yawn. "Bed? — Where have I heard that word before?"

"Don't ask me!" said Elder, yawning full, wide and unashamed.

21

W HEN in the course of the succeeding day the *Merchant Mariner* had worked her way well up into the area of the Iceland Patrol, Captain Elder relaxed his vigilance long enough to take a bath, change his clothes and sit down for a good, hot meal in the officers' saloon.

"I've been writing up my report, sir," Ensign O'Reilly was saying. "— My official account of the big scrap, I mean. I wonder if

you'd care to substantiate my claim that we shot
the periscope off that submarine?"

"Why not?" said Elder. "— Nobody's
going to sue us over a little thing like that! I bet
they just called in the plumber and had her fixed
as good as new in twenty minutes!"

"Well, maybe! But it was pretty good
shooting, you've got to admit that, sir!"

"Of course it was good shooting!"

"The Navy trains good shots!"

"Yunh? Well, if you should ask me, that
boy Goldberg had plenty of training with
machine guns before he ever heard of the Navy!
All the time he was shooting at that submarine,
he had his handkerchief wrapped around the
grips so's he wouldn't leave fingerprints."

Ensign O'Reilly looked at him uncer-
tainly. He was never quite sure whether Elder
was kidding or not. And with a man of Elder's
pyrotechnic temper, it was uncomfortable to
make mistakes.

"M'm, I see!" he murmured, noncommit-
tally. "Still, that's — that's hardly the sort of
thing I could put in my report, is it, sir?"

"No," said Captain Elder, "I suppose it
isn't. But if you're looking for some really hot

stuff to put in it — something with zing, zip, heart-interest, oomph, a sweater and a sarong — why don't you tell'em how Dashing Dave Elder, of the U.S. Merchant Marine, met a torpedo head on and shoved it off the sidewalk with his bow wave?"

Ensign O'Reilly inclined his head. "I have already covered the incident in my report, Captain," he said. "Er — as a matter of fact, I described it as the greatest feat of seamanship yet witnessed in this war."

"Eh? Hunh?" Now it was Elder's turn to be puzzled. "— Oh, hell, no — you didn't, really!"

"I certainly did, sir!" said Ensign O'Reilly, and it was plain that he spoke in earnest.

"M'm! M'mph!" Captain Elder's neck was scarlet with embarrassment. "Well, young feller-me-lad, I hope you learned a lesson from it, anyway! The next time you see anything come rushing at you — a torpedo, a wild bull, or — or a guy named Rocket Rockwell, for instance — all you gotta do is don't!"

"Don't what, sir?" inquired Ensign O'Reilly.

"Don't get your chin in the way!"
chuckled Captain Elder, reaching for the butter.

22

THERE followed uneventful days in which the *Merchant Mariner* plodded up between Iceland and the Faroes, then bore slightly eastward toward Norway — days which became longer and longer until only a few hours of red twilight separated one from another. For they were nearing the Arctic Circle, now, and in these latitudes, summer knows no night.

"Welp, I never seen nothin' so screwy as this!" declared One Round Kid Ahearn, resting his elbow on his machine gun and shading his eyes toward the half-disc of sun which was visible above the horizon. "Ten o'clock at night, time for the main bout to go on, and it's still too light to even start the prelims!"

"Well, you oughta know!" said Texas Fitch, spitting a gob of tobacco juice over the leeward side. "But I bet it was usually as light as this by the time you regained consciousness next morning, wasn't it?"

"Aw, lay off that stuff!" Hyman Goldberg interposed. "If the Kid's record of knockouts is all in the wrong column, it's only because he didn't have the right guy handling him, see? Now, you take most of these so-called managers and what have ya got? Why, ya got parasites, that's what ya got!"

"Unh-unh! Not me!" said Texas Fitch.

"— No, but what I mean! These guys'll tie up some poor stumble bum wit' a trick contract, pull down seventy or eighty per cent of the gross and never so much as lift a hand, see? But not me! Unh-unh! I earn my cut, I do! Ask any of my boys, and they'll tell ya I'm always there at the ringside, just the same as if I am right in there with 'em! Me, I really take care of my fighters! I woik for 'em! — I even think for 'em!"

"You even eat for 'em!" Texas added.

"— Hunh? — Eat?" One Round Ahearn pricked up his cauliflower cars. "Say, ain't it pretty near time for Jeff to bring up our Mocha and sandwitchers? I'm — I'm startin' to feel a little faint!"

"Just try to hang on till the bell, Kid!" Texas Fitch advised him. "If I was you, I ..."

"— Quiet, you guys!" Hyman Goldberg stood with his head tilted back and his eyes half-closed. "Listen! ... Listen! Can you hear it?"

"Hear what, Hymie?"

"That noise! That — that kind of a humming sound!"

"M'm ... — Reckon it's a generator or something, down in the engine room."

"It's the wind blow'n' through them stays."

"No, it's not! It sounds like a — like a plane! ... — There! — There! — Hear it now?"

"— M'm, yair! Yair! But say, that's funny! — I don't see no plane!'

171

For a moment they stood scanning the cloudless, pink-flushed sky; then Goldberg strode to the intercom telephone.

"Goldberg, sir!" he said into it. "We hear something that sounds like a plane, but ..."

"*Lookout aloft!*" a voice cut in on him. "A plane approaching on the port beam, sir! Flying very low, just skimming the water. He's maybe ten or twelve miles off, sir!"

"Okay! Watch for him, Goldberg!" O'Reilly ordered. "I'll be right up."

Goldberg swung his glasses and swept them along the horizon. "There he comes! There he comes! See him, Tex?"

"No. — Yes! Gosh, but he's low! — Just topping the waves, like a pelican!"

"Where is he? Where is he?" demanded Ensign O'Reilly breathlessly, joining them. "Oh, yes — I've got him! H'm — well, it's not an American plane, that's a cinch! No, and I don't think it's British ... If he'd only go up a bit higher so we could get a better silhouette ... Ah! There he zooms! He knows we've got him spotted! — Yes, by God, he's a German! — He's a Focke-Wulf!"

"Oh, he is, hunh!" Hyman Goldberg pulled down the arming lever of his machine gun and let it snap back, *ker-chuck!* "Okay, German! You're gettin' into the wrong territory!"

When the plane had reached an altitude of about a thousand feet, it circled around them, but stayed well out of range.

"He'll dive on us from astern," said O'Reilly. "He'll commence strafing us as soon as he starts down, and drop his bombs as he's passing over."

"'Passing over' is right!" said Texas Fitch, grimly. "In just about two minutes from now, he'll be passing over the River Jordan." He fell to singing a cowboy song about crossing the Jordan with his boots on.

Astern of them, the plane banked steeply and started down on an easy slant, its motors wide open. Suddenly, tracer bullets squirted from its nose like white-hot hornets. They whipped up the water, they drummed on the decks, they ricochetted off plates and winches and went crisscrossing one another, buzzing, whining, screaming ...

"Hold your fire, men!"

"Yes, sir!"

"Hyahs you cawfee and sandwiches, gents! — Nice and hot!"

"Jeff! Get out of here! Lie down! Lie down!"

"Cain't lay down, Mistah O'Reilly! Cain't spill this cawfee, suh!

"Here, Jeff! Git in back of me!" One Round Kid Ahearn shoved the pantryman behind him. The tray crashed to the deck.

"— He's getting ready to bomb! Watch out! Here they come!"

"Fire! Let 'em have it!"

As the .50 calibres went hammering into action, the *Merchant Mariner* trembled to a terrific explosion. A white column leaped mast-high beside her and then collapsed, deluging the decks in tons of falling water. An instant later, the plane's nose jerked violently upward, as though the pilot was deliberately trying to snap its wings off. The outer right hand motor burst into flame.

"Got him!" screamed Goldberg, squinting through his sights and continuing to pour bullets into the disabled plane. "Got him! Ah! There! There! There he goes!"

The great plane struck the water with a mighty splash, disintegrating under the impact. All that remained of her was a wing pontoon, a fragment of an aileron and a smear of oil on the sea.

Hyman Goldberg snapped down the safety on his gun, walked to the rail and surveyed the debris. Then he spat in its direction. "Okay, you smalltime Nazi punks!" he said. "I guess that'll learn ya not to muscle in on my territory!"

"Mistah O'Reilly, suh! Mistah O'Reilly, suh!"

"Yes, Jeff! What's the matter, boy — did they get you?"

"No, suh, but Ah — Ah cain't get out from under Mistah Ahearn!"

In a pitiful welter of coffee, sandwiches and his own blood, One Round Kid Ahearn lay sprawled across the shipmate he had died to save.

ACTION IN THE NORTH ATLANTIC

23

FROM the bridge, Captain Elder looked
down at the flag-covered coffin and the
three ranks of men formed around it
under the bombers on the well deck. Ensign
O'Reilly raised his head and saluted. "All ready,
Captain!" he called.

"Very well, Mr. Rossi you can stop her!"

The telegraph bell clanged dully in the
engine room and the smooth rumble of
machinery was stilled. As the ship lost way, one
heard the swish of water against her sides. She

came to a stop, swaying gently, and then the only sounds were the faint creaking of the hull, the whisper of the wind through the stays and the mewing of the snow-white Arctic gulls which circled lazily in the sunshine.

Prayer book in hand, Elder went slowly down the ladder. He removed his cap and took his place beside the coffin. For a moment he stood with his eyes closed, as though listening for something in the silence. Then he nodded, as though hearing it. He opened the prayer book and read — read with great feeling, for he was moved profoundly. His emotion was shared by his audience. He neared the end.

"... Forasmuch as it has pleased Almighty God of His great wisdom to take unto Himself the soul of our dear brother here departed, we therefore commend his body to the deep to be turned into corruption, looking forward for the resurrection of the body when the sea shall give up its dead."

He raised his hand.

"To God the Father, God the Son and God the Holy Ghost. Amen!"

The coffin slid forward on the trestles and disappeared over the side, the folds of the flag caressing it to the last. There was the sound of a splash.

Captain Elder drew a long breath and snapped his prayer book closed. Then he turned and looked up at the bridge.

"Okay, Mr. Rossi — get her under way!"

The telegraph bell clanged dully in the engine room. The machinery took up its smooth rumble. The *Merchant Mariner* resumed her pilgrimage to Murmansk.

ACTION IN THE NORTH ATLANTIC

24

L ATER that day, Jeff Caldwell was seated
at the pantry table, polishing
spoons, but his heart was not in his
work. As he dropped them one by one into the
drawer — "He died for me!" he repeated over
and over, as though unable to believe it. "A man
— a white man — died for me! Of course, Ah
know a White Man died for all of us and His
blessed name was Jesus. But Ah — Ah never
expected, Ah nevah dreamed, a white man
would die for me — puhsonally!"

But presently he nodded and sat up straight, as though convinced of something. "Yes, it's true! It's exactly like Stanislawski said! A colored boy has got a chance in America, same as anybody else! It's simply up to me to make the most of mah opportunity! Er — Er — *Hello, Mistah Benny — this is ... this is....*"

Jeff Caldwell buried his face in his hands and wilted to the table, sobbing.

The inter-com telephone in the wheel-house jangled. Elder, who was nearest, picked it up. "Bridge! — Commanding Officer!" he said. Simultaneously he heard O'Reilly's voice come in: "Gun platform!"

"*Lookout aloft!*" the caller identified himself. "There's a small dark floating object dead ahead! — About three miles. — Looks like a life raft, sir!"

"Right! Keep your eye on it and report!" ordered O'Reilly, promptly and completely taking charge of the situation. "All other lookout stations! Ignore object ahead and watch your own sectors only! — This may be a trap! — Captain Elder! Change course fifteen degrees to port, so I can bring the gun to bear.

Vary speed from FULL AHEAD to DEAD SLOW every thirty seconds and stand ready to dodge torpedoes!"

As the vessel cautiously approached the raft, it became apparent that its passengers were in sore distress. One of them, utterly succumbed, lay sprawled on his face with his arm dangling in the water. The other, propped up on his elbow, continued to make feeble beckoning signs until the effort became too much for him; then he, too, collapsed.

"Poor devils!" said Elder. "— They're too far gone to catch a line. — You'll have to lower a boat and pick them up, Mr. Rossi."

"Okay, sir!" The mate blew his whistle and tightened his life jacket. "All right, you guys! — Man Number One boat!"

Shortly, the castaways were picked up, the lifeboat was hoisted to its davits and the ship put back on her course. Elder left the bridge and went aft to the sick bay, where he found Jeff reviving the sufferers with hot rum and coffee.

"Ach, Captain!" whispered the taller of the two, and even in his present plight it was apparent that he was an officer. "Captain! I cannot begin to tell you how grateful we are!

183

Seventy-two hours we have floated on that raft since the damned submarine sunk us! Seventy-two hours we … Ach, but pardon me, Captain!" He sat up feebly and bowed. "I must to introduce myself! — I am Captain Cornelius Eckhout, until three days ago Master of the Nederland Oostzee Company's motorship *Amersfoort*, of Flushing!" He bowed again, this time less feebly.

"Well, you've had plenty hard luck, Captain Eckhout! My name's Elder," he extended his hand. "— You're on the *Merchant Mariner*, U. S. Maritime Commission, New York to Murmansk."

"Murmansk! Ah, to be sure! Well, I did not expect to be going back there quite so soon. But, God-be-thanked!, I had delivered my cargo — agricultural chemicals and hospital supplies from England — and was on the way back empty when the — the dirty Nazi pigs sent my ship to the bottom!"

"Well, it's a good job you'd delivered the stuff, anyway! But say — who's this other poor chap? He seems to be pretty badly used up!"

"— He? Oh, he is one of my crew." He reached across to the other cot and shook the sailor.

"What's your name?" he asked, in Dutch.

"Anton Falck, *Mijnheer.*"

"Can you speak English?"

"Yes, Captain."

"Well, speak it then. This gentleman is an American officer. What's your birthplace, Falck?"

"Haarlem, sir."

Elder patted him on the shoulder. "— Okay, Falck — don't try to sit up. — You stay right where you are until you feel better. — Captain Eckhout, there's a cabin next to mine that I'm sure you'll be comfortable in."

"Ach, dear sir, you are too kind, too amiable!" said Captain Eckhout, effusively.

"Not at all, not at all! When you've rested a little, just ring for Jeff and he'll show you up to it."

Action in the North Atlantic

25

THE Dutchmen recovered in a day or so and then, with commendable spirit, proceeded to do whatever they could to make themselves useful on the ship. Because neither Elder nor any of his officers were familiar with the North Cape waters, they were glad to avail themselves of Captain Eckhout's considerable knowledge. Falck, who had served in the Dutch navy, volunteered to stand regular lookout watch with the gun crew, thus replacing the dead Ahearn.

"Myself, I am taking what our English friends would call a busman's holiday," Eckhout explained. "This marvelous American ship — your modern American methods — all are to me a revelation! I am studying everything. Now, I go to the chart room, to learn what new wrinkles I can of the navigation."

"Fine!" said Elder. "Just continue to make yourself at home, Captain."

In the chart room, Eckhout was greeted by Mr. Blair. "Well, Captain, only four days more to Murmansk! — That is, if the weather holds ..."

"Ah, yes, the weather! — In these latitudes, that is always the uncertain factor." The Dutchman considered the barometer, then the sky, and shrugged. "I would predict a storm," he said. "— Perhaps later today." He leaned over the chart, on which the vessel's track was indicated by a line connecting a series of little pencilled crosses. "Does Captain Elder intend to hold to the present course?"

"Yes. He figures that the farther north we stay, the less chance there is of tangling with the Nazi planes from Petsamo."

"A very wise precaution," said Captain Eckhout. "But as for the weather —" he consulted the chronometer and set his wristwatch by it, "— Well, I am afraid it will be bad tonight."

And he was right. By seven o'clock, black clouds piled up on the northern horizon. By nine, a sleet-laden gale set in, whipping the crests off the waves and driving them across the plunging *Merchant Mariner* in a blinding smother of spray.

Mr. Rossi turned to Captain Elder, who had joined him on the bridge, and shouted to make himself heard above the tumult of the storm. "Gosh, some night! First time it's been dark for two weeks!"

"Yes, and thank God for it! No need to worry about planes tonight — nor subs either, with the sea that's running ... Er, yes, Johnson? What is it?"

"Sparks is missing, sir!" announced the Assistant Operator, cupping his hands and leaning against the wind. "I went in to relieve him and he wasn't there."

"Hell! Have you searched the ship?"

"Yes, sir, we've been all over it. He just isn't aboard."

"— D'you hear that, Joe?"

"Yes. — Looks like he'd had another one of his crazy spells."

"— And jumped overboard? Say, I'm afraid that's just what's happened!" He peered out into the raging darkness and shook his head. "Well, Johnson, there's nothing we can do now. — Get back on the job and we'll see what we can find out in the morning. Maybe he left a note or something."

But next day, when the storm had abated and Spark's quarters were searched, no note or other evidence of premeditation was found. It was generally concluded that he had acted on a sudden, fear-crazed impulse. "He even had his pajamas layed out on his bunk, so he could hit the hay as soon as he came off watch," Parker reported, at breakfast. "I bet he tuned in that Hamburg Nazi again, got the wah-wahs listening to the 'death knell' and ..." He made a grimace, "Well, the poor kid!"

"Ach, yes, it is a very sad business!" said Captain Eckhout, nodding grimly. "Not only do these accursed Nazis kill with torpedos and bombs; they kill by destroying the mind. And against that sort of warfare there is no armor, no defense! None!"

"Well, yes, Captain, I think there is," said Elder. "The armor, the defense, is faith. — Or at least, it saved a fellow countryman of yours at the bombing of Rotterdam." He repeated Captain Vanderhoven's story as he had heard it in Halifax, that night (was it a year, or could it be only a month ago?) before the convoy sailed. "— And so," he concluded, "And so, when the bomb struck his home, poor Vanderhoven had nothing left. — Nothing, that is, except his reason, and a faith strong enough to protect it. In a word, he had God."

Captain Eckhout, who had listened intently, inclined his head. "I respect your friend," he said. "I, too, was in Rotterdam that day, and even for me, who suffered no personal calamity, it was an ordeal almost to shatter the mind. Ach! Never was a more savage atrocity committed in all the history of the world! With my own eyes, I saw the white rockets shoot up in token of surrender — and one minute, two minutes later, there came the Stukas screaming! — And the bombs! Ach, the bombs!" He covered his face with his hands and swayed slowly back and forth. Then, recovering himself — "Pray forgive me, gentlemen! The memory of that — that awful day will be with me always!" He rose, bowed stiffly and left the room.

26

ELDER nodded after him sympathetically. "The memory'll always be with him, yes — but it'll always be with him wrong. It just goes to show what an experience of that kind can do to a man!"

"What do you mean, Dave?"

"Why, those rockets he saw at Rotterdam weren't white at all. They were red," said Captain Elder.

"If you should ask me, it's about time we saw some Russian planes," Mr. Rossi observed next morning, scanning the sky to the southward.

"If you should ask me, it's about time we delivered 'em some," said Captain Elder, indicating the Lockheeds on the deck below. "I wonder how many of the other ships ..."

"Submarine! Port Beam!"

Like a whale with water pouring off its back, the sub was surfacing. She was less than a mile away.

"My God!" Elder gasped. "Is he crazy? Is he trying to commit suicide? He must be English or — but no! No! He's German, all right!"

Even before the submarine's length was completely exposed, WHAM! the *Merchant Mariner's* four-inch gun blazed away at her. The shot fell wide. So did the next, and the next.

"Hell, what shooting!" Elder screamed, pounding the rail with his fist. "What's the matter with those fellows back there?"

WHAM! WHAM! WHAM! The shooting now was even wilder than before.

Very calmly, men appeared on the submarine's forward deck. Her gun flashed. An instant later, the *Merchant Mariner* winced under a shattering explosion. The upper half of her funnel came crashing to the starboard deck, lay teetering for a moment in a cloud of soot, smoke and steam and then slid over the side with a mighty splash, taking the splintered lifeboats with it.

Elder sprang to the phone. "O'Reilly! O'Reilly! What's the matter, man? Why don't you ..." There was another explosion aft — just where, Elder was unable to see through the smoke. The phone went dead.

"You!" he bawled to the .50 calibre crew behind the bridge, "Get busy with those machine guns! Cut loose! Let'em have it!"

There was a series of muffled pops, as from wet firecrackers, followed by cries of pain and frenzied cursing. Then, silence.

"What happened, Parker — can you see?"

"The guns exploded, sir! All four of 'em! As soon as they squeezed the triggers they — they simply blew to hell!"

Elder hunched his shoulders and licked his lips. "We've got to run for it! Rossi, phone the Engine Room to give her everything she's got!"

The submarine fired again. This time, the shell splashed directly in the vessel's path. "He wants us to stop! Well, by God, we won't stop!"

Ensign O'Reilly appeared, pressing a bloody hand to his side. "Captain! " he gasped, leaning against the wheelhouse, "The sight ... on the gun ... was all cockeyed, sir! Somebody'd ... bent it ... out of line ... And the machine guns ... the barrels all blew up ... Somebody'd ... somebody'd ..." With a thin sigh, he wilted to the deck.

PLOSH! Another shell plunged into the water just ahead of them.

"He's keeping up with us! What's the matter with those fellows in the engine room, Rossi?"

"They say they can't keep pressure, sir. — Some pipes are busted. — Look at all that steam escaping by the funnel!"

The submarine cut toward them on a long diagonal, a bone in her teeth. Soon, she was running with them neck and neck, a scant two hundred yards away. An officer in her conning tower waved his arms in threatening admonition and then levelled a megaphone.

"Stop at once, fool!" he bellowed. "Stop! Lower a boat and put Kapitan von Stoeffer aboard us unharmed, or we'll drown every man on the ship!"

"Captain Who? What the hell's he talking about?" barked Elder. "But — okay!" He sprang to the wheel. "Okay! If the swine wants me to put somebody aboard him, I'll put the whole damned ship aboard him! I'll ..."

"Careful, Captain!" the low voice of Captain Cornelius Eckhout came from close behind him. "This — metal object which you feel against your ribs is your own pistol, my dear Captain!"

"Hunh? Why, you — you!..."

"Now, don't get excited, Captain — and don't show it if you do! Remember, you and your ship are utterly helpless! Ach, utterly! So please ask Mr. Rossi to ring off the engines and ..."

Elder's right elbow drove back and caught him in the stomach. He heard a shot and felt something rip through his shoulder. Cadet Parker threw himself upon the German, then fell back coughing with a bullet in his chest. Before the fellow could fire again, Rossi knocked him down, stamped on his hand and broke his jaw with a kick.

With his unwounded arm, Elder spun the wheel full left. From somewhere aft came shouts and the pound of running feet, but he heard the sounds dimly, if at all. For now, the *Merchant Mariner's* bow was swinging toward the submarine. — Now she was heading straight for it. A shell struck her starboard anchor and drove it back into the chain locker. Through the smoke, Elder could see the Germans standing fear frozen at their gun. The sub swerved. Elder chuckled and shoved down the wheel. The *Merchant Mariner's* mighty steel snout was aimed directly at the conning tower.

There was a crash, a shock which caused the ship to stagger. For an instant her bow rose, as though she were trying to climb out of water, and from under her forefoot came an agonized, deafening, head-filling CRUNCH! Then, abruptly, she settled down again, like a canoe which had slid over a sunken log. On either side of her, a jagged-edged half of the submarine rolled and wallowed soggily, then plunged out of sight in belching, boiling foam. From out of the foam came a foul smell.

Elder rang off the engines and ran to the rail. "Well, well, well, boys!" he yelled at the Germans struggling in the welter of oil and muck. "Don't tell me you've been rammed! — You have? Well, well, well — how do you like it? — Fun, eh? Oh, sure, it's just great, isn't it? Come on, boys — enjoy yourselves! Let's hear you sing! — Let's see you wave! — Let's see you thumb your noses! Don't you want me to take your picture?"

The Germans were making imploring gestures.

"What's that? Oh, so you don't like it, eh? — So it's different, when you're on the receiving end, is it? Well, just be patient a minute, boys, and we'll drag you out and cheat the fishes! Er — Mr. Rossi!" he turned. "Where's Mr. Rossi?"

"He just left the bridge, sir. He had this fellow's pistol."

"Oh! Well, send the carpenter down into the forepeak, Mr. Blair, to see if she's taking in any water. Then lower a boat and see how many of those rats you can pick up." He stumbled over the Nazi, who was lying on his back, his eyes glassy and his broken jaw jutting sideways. "Oh, pardon me, my dear Herr Kapitan Von What's-your-name! — Been seeing any more white rockets, lately?"

Painfully and with great effort, the Nazi spat up at him. The spittle fell back in his own face.

"Ha! — Pleasant specimen, aren't you?" said Elder.

Suddenly his shoulder hurt. It hurt terribly. He saw that the entire right side of his uniform was soaked with blood. He was not quite sure about all that had happened and trying to remember it made his temples throb. He felt dizzy.

He turned to a sailor. "This fellow ... shot Johnny Parker, too ... didn't he?" he asked, dully.

"Yes, sir."

"Is Parker hurt bad?"

"Very bad, sir. — He shot him through the lungs."

Elder looked down at the battered Nazi. "If I had my gun, I'd ... I'd ram it down your throat and ..."

Just then a shot rang out below.

"What's that?"

The sailor moved to the rail and looked down at the well deck. "It's Mr. Rossi, sir. He just bumped off that other German!"

"Ah? Good!" Elder swayed against the telegraph and grasped it for support. "Please ... help me ... to my room."

ACTION IN THE NORTH ATLANTIC

27

"HOW'RE you feeling, Dave?"

"Oh, I had a good enough night. But tell me, Joe — how're Parker and O'Reilly?"

"O'Reilly's okay. But Johnny," Mr. Rossi's lip trembled, "Johnny — shoved off — about ten minutes ago. He wiped his eyes on the back of his hand. "Just before he died, he — he asked me to post this for him."

Elder blinked through his tears at the bloodstained envelope. "Miss Mary Pollard, Route 3, Glorietta, Cherokee County, Kansas,

U. S. A." He read the address as though he were reading the burial service.

Mr. Rossi rose, shoved his hands into his pockets and stood at the porthole, gazing out upon the bleak wave-pounded granite cliffs and gloomy fir forests of the Murman coast. For a long time the pair were silent. Then Elder cleared his throat. "Well!" he said huskily, "Well!"

"Well, Dave — I guess that's that!" said Mr. Rossi.

"How many prisoners have we got?"

"Eighteen, counting the one whose jaw I broke. It seems a Russian destroyer sunk his sub five or six hours before we came along and was damned fool enough to drop him that life raft. Well, while I was at it, I wish to God I'd killed him!"

"Yes, Joe, I wish you had. How come you killed the other one?"

"Oh, him! Well, I had him cornered and he had his hands up, hollering 'Kamerad!' But as soon as I came near him to put the irons on, he brought one hand down, ker-swack, and — well, he had a sandbag in it!" Mr. Rossi felt his left shoulder gingerly.

"A sandbag?"

"Yair — made out of a woolen sock. It must have been what he used to slug Sparks with, before they chucked him overboard and sent off their message. He got the sand out of a fire bucket. O'Reilly says there was at least a handful of it in the barrel of each of the machine guns, too."

"Gosh! No wonder they blew up!"

"Yes — and the way that sight on the after gun was bent, it was no wonder O'Reilly kept missing the sub."

"Well, by gosh, it was pretty smart of 'em, Joe! — Smart, the German way."

"What do you mean, smart the German way?"

"Why, I mean that the Germans are always smart enough to think up ways of causing trouble, but they're never quite smart enough to get any thing out of it. That's why they don't win wars!"

ACTION IN THE NORTH ATLANTIC

28

OUTSIDE Naval Headquarters, on Murmansk's Square of the Revolution, a great crowd was gathered. In the center of this crowd, within a hollow square of Russian and American bluejackets and marines, Vice-Admiral Igor Stolypin, Commander-in-Chief of the Northern Red Fleet, was conferring the Order of Afansy Matushenko the Sailor upon Captain David Elder. The Admiral was eloquent, but because his English was peculiar, a considerable portion of his audience, including Elder, had only the sketchiest notion of what he was talking about.

"Jeece!" said little Smitty, standing on tiptoe and viewing the proceedings between the shoulders of two stalwart Russian girls. "Look at the Old Man blush! I bet there's plenty of places he'd rather be than here!"

"Him and me both!" said handsome Stan Stanislawski, whose attention had been straying. "F'r instance, just get a load of them two blonde chickadees standing right in front of you, Smitty! Looka the eyes on 'em! Looka the shapes on 'em! Oh, boy, oh boy! If I could only talk Russian, I'd ..."

One of the ladies wheeled upon him. "Oh, ya would, wouldja? Well, you louse, take THAT!"

Stanislawski retreated in poor order, his hand pressed to his smarting cheek. Glancing fearfully behind him, he saw that Smitty had moved in between the damsels and had an arm around the waist of each of them. The trio were chatting and laughing gaily.

Admiral Stolypin wound up his discourse in a whirlwind of oratory and pinned the medal on Elder's breast. Then, embracing him carefully, so as not to hurt his wounded shoulder, he planted a whiskery kiss on either cheek. There was a fanfare of bugles and a rattle of rifles as the guard presented arms.

Then Admiral William Lacey, U.S.N., stepped forward and saluted Elder. "Captain," he said, "in congratulating you upon the high honor just bestowed by the Soviet Government, I am privileged to inform you that your own Government, as well, has taken cognizance of the heroic and invaluable services which you have rendered. The full story of your gallantry was contained in the official report of Ensign O'Reilly, of your gun crew, which was transmitted to Washington and given careful study. As a result, in behalf of the Congress of the United States of America, and by its direction, I now present you with the nation's highest award — the Congressional Medal of Honor."

With the band playing and the American and Russian naval staffs lined up behind him, Elder stood in a daze as the guard marched past him at the salute. He was still in a daze as a naval lieutenant rushed up to him, grasped his good hand and cried,

"Congratulations, Pop!"

"Hunh? Howard! Howard! Why, hello there, Howard! How are you, boy?"

"Fine, Pop! I ..."

"M'mph! Now, now! Don't call me Pop!"

"All right, then — GRANDPOP!"

"Hunh? What's that? — You — you mean Adelaide's going to have a ? ..."

"Yop! Got a letter on the plane that came in this morning!"

"Well, I'll be ...!"

"— Say, Pop — if it's a boy, what'll we do with him? — Put him in the Navy or in the Merchant Marine?"

"H'm!" Elder stroked his chin thoughtfully. "Gosh, Howard," he said, "Won't it be great if he's — twins?"